SILVER CREEK TRAIL

In Silver Creek, it seemed that Dan Lawrence had been involved with two successive shooting deaths. So there was little wonder when he panicked and took off for parts unknown. His employer, Hector Morissey, had guaranteed Dan's appearance in court with $10,000, which he now stood to lose. Morissey's detective brother, Ed, went after Dan, risking his life against the bullets of Dan's outlaw associates. But Dan's final determination to do what was right made it all worthwhile.

Books by David Bingley
in the Linford Western Library:

THE BEAUCLERC BRAND
ROGUE'S REMITTANCE
STOLEN STAR
BRIGAND'S BOUNTY
TROUBLESHOOTER ON TRIAL
GREENHORN GORGE
RUSTLERS' MOON
SUNSET SHOWDOWN
TENDERFOOT TRAIL BOSS
HANGTOWN HEIRESS
HELLIONS' HIDEAWAY
THE JUDGE'S TERRITORY
KILLERS' CANYON
SIX-SHOOTER JUNCTION
THE DIAMOND KID
RED ROCK RENEGADES
HELLIONS AT LARGE
BUZZARD'S BREED
REDMAN RANGE
LAWMAN'S LAMENT
THE COYOTE KIDS
BRIGAND'S BLADE

DAVID BINGLEY

---◆---

SILVER CREEK TRAIL

Complete and Unabridged

LINFORD
Leicester

First published in Great Britain in 1971

First Linford Edition
published 2007

The moral right of the author has been asserted

British Library CIP Data

Bingley, David, *1920 –*
    Silver creek trail.—Large print ed.—
    Linford western library
    1. Western stories
    2. Large type books
    I. Title
    823.9'14 [F] 749 7433

    ISBN 978-1-84617-850-4

Published by
F. A. Thorpe (Publishing)
Anstey, Leicestershire

Set by Words & Graphics Ltd.
Anstey, Leicestershire
Printed and bound in Great Britain by
T. J. International Ltd., Padstow, Cornwall

This book is printed on acid-free paper

1

The small western town of Silver Creek, in the south of Rockland County, New Mexico territory, was alive with merry-making. At ten o'clock in the evening, when the sun was dipping down in the west, the one-time saloon which was known as the Old Barn, was spilling the sounds of music and laughter, and the smells of good food and strong drink.

A three-piece orchestra consisting of a violinist, a pianist and a concertina player, was turning out a lively rhythm to which upwards of thirty couples were whirling and dancing. The dancers' pounding feet were knocking the dust out of the worn floorboards and at the same time adding to the catchy beat of the tune.

From a point just inside the batwing doors, Ed Morissey, a tall fair young man in his late twenties, was surveying the couples on the dance floor and at the same time unconsciously tapping his foot. He had a small cigar in his hand, and from time to time he raised it to his lips and drew upon it.

Ed's business in life was that of a detective. He was a natural observer, and not much that was going on in the room missed his eyes.

On a small raised-up dais at the far end, the trio in the orchestra were working hard. The elderly fiddler, playing in his shirt sleeves, was beginning to perspire and to find it difficult to keep up with the rhythm as the other two played.

Two youngsters in their late teens were examining with polite interest a table full of gun belts and hand guns, surrendered by the male dancers as they entered the building. Men and women were sitting in wooden arm-chairs around the walls, watching the antics of those more energetic than themselves. In an alcove on one side of the room was a table spread with glasses and a big container of a powerful punch. Yet another alcove contained a long table with an assortment of food, cold meats and sandwiches.

Presently, the dance rhythm came to a crescendo and then stopped. While the master of ceremonies pushed his way through the many couples who did not bother to clear the floor, the old fiddler went over to the piano and thirstily gulped down a half pint of beer.

'Ladies and gents, your attention, please. I'd like all the ladies to form a circle in the middle of the floor and all the gents to form another circle around them. When the marching music stops, the gents will take as their partners the ladies who are nearest to them in the line. Until the marching music starts again. You all know the kind of dance this is, it's to make folks mix, so let's have a good response an' if you don't want to dance this time, be good enough to move off the floor. Thank you.'

While the musicians toyed with their instruments, Ed Morissey turned to a wall and examined himself in a long mirror. He was lean of face and blue-eyed, and on this occasion he was dressed in a brown corduroy jacket, dark trousers and half boots. A bright red necktie contrasted with the deep blue of his shirt.

He was satisfied with his appearance, and he hurriedly stepped into the circle of men as the music started up. There were several really pretty girls in the women's circle, but Ed's eyes were only for one of them, a shapely green-eyed girl with long copper-coloured hair who looked radiant in a long billowing gown of bottle green velvet. She was Pearl Winder, a local beauty of twenty and the only child of an ageing rancher and his wife who kept a watchful eye on her and also upon those who paid attention to her.

The marching music stopped and there was a pause. Ed found himself graciously accepting as a partner the flat-footed wife of a homesteader who weighed as much as himself, if not more. He was glad when the music changed again. He attempted and succeeded in catching the eye of the copper-headed girl.

She called: 'Howdy, Ed, how are you making out for partners?'

Before he could answer in a suitable fashion they were too far apart to hear one another and he felt that a small opportunity to make contact had been missed. After two more changes of routine, he was lucky enough to find Pearl right opposite to him when the music stopped and the couples paired off.

He was only just in time in taking her in his arms. Alongside of him, Dan Lawrence, a young redhead, recently returned to town, pulled back with a frown on his face and reluctantly accepted as his partner a thin lean woman with a tight bun of greying hair.

The new music was a waltz, and Pearl appeared to float in Ed's arms as he steered her round the floor.

He said: 'I've been tryin' to get close to you all evenin', Pearl, but you seem to have more beaux than any girl in the place. It ain't rightly fair, you know. A man like me, whose brother is a lawyer, doesn't want to get involved in a fist fight to get next to his favourite girl. You ought to do something about it.'

Pearl giggled and then laughed out loud, showing a fine mouthful of small white teeth. Dancers and sitters in all directions turned towards Ed and the girl, drawn by the laughter. Ed felt good to know that she was in his arms when she was attracting so much attention, but her next words did not build up his hopes for the evening.

'Why, Ed, I do believe you're jealous of the boys who pay me attention! Jealousy suits you, it puts a little extra colour in your face. But you must not build up your hopes for tonight, buddy boy, because I have a dance programme an' every single dance is spoken for. I'll show you the programme, if you like!'

The girl's face was full of mocking

laughter, but Ed felt he could stand it. At least she knew how he felt about her, and she was not indifferent to him. He released her with great reluctance when the music changed and danced with two other partners before the dance came to an end.

After escorting a tradesman's wife back to her husband, Ed made a half circle round the room and helped himself to a glass of punch. He sipped it, and went on with his survey of the other people. Pearl had gone back to the spot where her mother and father were sitting.

The start of a new dance saw the keen young men on their feet and moving off to pick up the women of their choice. Ed felt a new pang of jealousy as he saw Dan Lawrence stroll importantly over to the Winder group and bow to the old couple before returning to the floor with Pearl's hand resting on his arm.

Dan was just twenty-two years of age. He had returned to town a short time before after completing two years in a Tennessee law school. In fact, he had joined the law firm of Ed's older brother, Hector, further along the Main Street. Mervin Hayes, who had married Dan's mother and taken over the Diamond L ranch, had paid the money to keep Dan at law school, but rumour had it that Mervin, who was tight-fisted, had no intention of spending any more money upon his stepson's career.

Dan was a bright, but rather headstrong young man. He had a backsliding nose and rather small features. The expression on his face which most people saw was an ingenuous one, but it could easily turn to a frown, and many of the older people in the Old Barn were of the opinion that he was immature for his age, even if he was a qualified lawyer.

Music again filled the warm room, and the keen couples started their dancing. Dan and Pearl were among the first. It was clear by the way Mr. and Mrs. Winder were nodding and smiling that they fully approved of their daughter being in the company of young Lawrence.

Ed watched the couple rather sadly as they appeared and disappeared from view amid the other dancers. Dan's reappearance in the town reminded Ed of the fact that he, too, had taken some training in law school. But Ed had come away from the school when his training was only half over. His general restlessness had made him break away and set himself up as a detective instead of sticking it out and qualifying as a fully-fledged lawyer.

Dan had done, in fact, what Ed ought to have done. Having been back a few years, Ed was now of the opinion that he ought to have finished his training instead of throwing in his hand. After all, he need not have practised if the work of an attorney had proved too dull.

He had learned that the acquiring of professional status gave a man a lot of prestige in a western town. Many other mature townsfolk had shown their approval of the Lawrence young man since his return, and many of these same people looked down upon Ed as a failed lawyer, a man who had started up as a private detective in a makeshift occupation.

Ed yawned. He moved around and chatted with a couple of shopkeepers whose only aim was to have a good time.

Pearl and Dan parted. In the next few dances, others commandeered the pretty girl's attention. And then Dan was back with her, and Ed was beginning to feel bored as well as frustrated. He made excuses to the men with whom he was talking and sauntered towards the main entrance.

At the table where the firearms had been stacked, Reg Yarby, a good-hearted stable hand who was in charge of the weapons, called out to Ed, all the while stroking his flecked grey beard.

'Hey, Ed, this is early for you to be goin' home. Are you sayin' you've had enough already, 'cause if you are you'd better take your hog's leg an' gun belt offen this pile.'

Ed grinned at Reg, and gave him a small cigar. 'Leave it for now, Reg. I might be back for another short session. Right now I'm keener on gettin' fresh air than anything else.'

Yarby nodded and chuckled. 'Lots of folks have the same idea, Ed, but they're using the other door. I reckon it would be hard to find a nice sparkin' spot down by the creek right now which hasn't already been taken!'

Ed nodded and gave an answer of no particular consequence. As he glanced towards the other door at the far end of the building, he saw Pearl Winder on the point of slipping out of doors in the company of Dan Lawrence. He figured that Dan was having all the luck tonight. Would he always stay popular when he had been back in the town for some time? There he was, going off to the creek with the town's prettiest girl, and her parents were acting as though

11

they approved even that.

It surely looked as if the Winders wanted a lawyer for a son-in-law.

Reg was about to remark upon the young couple's departure, but Ed hastily cut him short and pushed through the batwings into the fresh air. In the darkness, his lean face wore the sort of expression which would have given away the depth of his true feelings.

He surely felt bad about Pearl going out to spark with a young whippersnapper like Dan Lawrence. Why, he was little more than a boy!

Ed began to walk the boards. He increased his speed and did not stop until he was outside a small *cantina* run by a friendly Mexican on the outskirts of town. Inside, the atmosphere was less charged with excitement. The lights were dimmer. The beer was warm, but he took two glasses and drank them down with obvious enjoyment before passing the time of day with the proprietor and starting the walk back.

The Old Barn was less than a

hundred yards away when the staccato crackle of gun shots carried to him from the direction of the creek. He paused in his walk, expecting more, but all he heard after that were the echoes. And then a woman screamed. One young woman screaming at a distance sounded much like another, but his first thoughts were about Pearl. Had she screamed, and was she involved in the shooting? If so, Ed had little confidence in her escort to give her protection.

He turned off down an alley, crossed two more streets at the run, and finally came out on the downward path which led from town into the wooded slope above the creek. This was the town's lovers' walk.

As he ran, he reflected that all the men coming from the dance with girls ought to be still without their revolvers. But perhaps the people from the Old Barn had nothing to do with the occurrence. He went on trying to reason it out, but his instinct told him that someone from the dance hall was in some way involved.

On the downward path he went more slowly, and acted warily. A man who had used a weapon once could easily use it again, if the balance of his mind was disturbed. The path forked into three different routes. At the junction, the young detective listened. He could faintly hear a girl sobbing, but it was difficult to pin down the direction.

Acting upon impulse, he took the middle path. Between twenty and thirty yards further along it, just as he ducked to avoid a protruding tree branch, he made his discovery. He could have done the same had he been blindfolded because the inert body was stretched directly across the path.

Ed caught his boot somewhere near the fallen man's waistline and pitched over him in a graceful arc. He banged his shoulder against the bole of a tree and swore briefly. His first reaction was to roll away and take cover, but the body over which he had fallen was never likely to move again of its own

14

volition. It was a corpse. From all fours, Ed moved lightly to his feet, standing beside the tree and testing the atmosphere, almost animal-like, in case there was a prowler near.

No one moved nearby. It appeared that the recent gun shots had silenced even the small sounds of nature. He had a false impression that the waters of the creek stood still.

Eventually, as other people from town began to filter through the streets to find out what had happened, Ed felt around in his pockets and produced a long match. It blossomed easily and illuminated the still face of the dead man. The head and features were quite distinctive. They belonged to a man of fifty. The small dark eyes were still open, and the lower part of the face was hidden behind a black closely-trimmed beard and moustache.

This was one Skinner Kopak, a solitary man who always wandered about in a half-length plaid coat. He was a known Peeping Tom.

2

Ed stood up, thinking about the true character of the dead man. Kopak had been a barber by profession. He knew his business, and shaved and cut hair to everyone's satisfaction, but he had few friends. The known nature of his peeping had been mostly secretive observations of what went on in lighted buildings. He had the habit of standing about in the dark and looking through windows.

The position in which he had now been found, however, seemed to suggest that he had also been in the habit of watching the antics of young lovers as well. Those small dark eyes, which would never see again, must have been very effective in the dark, otherwise a visit to the creek on an evening when there was little moonlight would have been fruitless to a curious-minded individual.

A young couple, poised and whispering not very far away, distracted Ed's thoughts. He turned in the direction of the voices and perceived that the other people were a little further down the same path as he was on.

He called out. 'Hey, you two down there! Who are you?'

There was a brief hesitation before he received an answer. The voice of the young man sounded strained.

'It's — I'm Billy Meehan an' I have Annie Rose with me. Annie's scared. Is it safe to come up that way? Who are you?'

Ed cleared his throat. He had placed the couple. Billy was a slightly bow-legged youngster who worked around the cattle spreads as a waddy. Annie Rose was the tall gawky daughter of a tradesman.

'This is Ed Morissey. Sure, it's all right to come on up now. I figure the gunman has moved on. But take a grip of yourself 'cause a man has been shot. He's lyin' here dead.'

Annie made a noise as though she was choking back a scream. Shortly afterwards, moving very slowly and holding hands very tightly, Billy and Annie came into view and halted some six feet away from the corpse. They were a little too far away to see clearly who it was, but neither of them wanted a closer look.

'It's Skinner Kopak, an' he died with bullets in the chest. So don't go worryin' yourself unduly, huh? Are there any more kids down by the creek?'

Billy seemed to have lost his tongue, but when Ed stared fixedly at him he made an effort to answer. 'No, I don't think so, Ed. When the shootin' happened, they all skedaddled. I figure they went in all directions. Nobody stayed around. Annie an' me, we were sittin' out on a log, over the water. Otherwise, we'd have been clear before now.'

The young couple were anxious to get out of the atmosphere of the trees in favour of the buildings, but Ed detained them a little longer.

'Tell me, before you go. Did you hear any shoutin' or see anything which would help us to find out who did the shootin'?'

Annie gulped, fingered her neck and answered round-eyed. 'Right after the shootin' there was someone running alongside of the creek, along that path, you know, a little further upstream. But don't ask us to go along there right now, will you, Mr. Morissey?'

Ed relaxed a little. He shook his head. 'No, I wouldn't want you to do that. Get away up to the Old Barn, an' if you see anything of the marshal tell him where to find the body. Me, I'll go take a look along that path you spoke of, see if I can find anything. So off you go an' do as I say.'

Ed nodded to them. He turned on his heel and went off down the path. Billy and the girl glanced after him. Seemingly they had expected him to stand by the corpse until someone else arrived. The couple glanced furtively at Skinner's body and then leapt over it and went up the path in a hurry.

Weeping willows grew in abundance along the creek bank. Their drooping branches and low foliage made a useful screen for sweethearts who wanted to be alone. At that time, however, the whole area was deserted and even to a man with nerves like Ed the area seemed a little on the sinister side, in the light of what had just happened.

Men's voices were coming distinctly now from the top of the slope where the path started downwards. The killer, unless he was hanging about seeking trouble, would be a goodly distance away from the scene of his crime.

Ed moved slowly, studying the shadows, and as he moved he wished he had his own bone-handled Colt strapped to his waist. He felt vulnerable. Nevertheless he pressed on. The creekside path meandered in and out, went up and down. It was when he topped a small rise that he first caught sight of the gun lying in the lush grass and fern beside the path.

His instincts warned him to be wary. Was it placed there as a trap to get his attention? Was the killer scheming to get behind him? Or had the weapon merely been discarded when the killer had finished with it?

His heart thumped hard as he drew aside and thoroughly checked the area. After a pause of about two minutes, he steeled himself to bend down and pick up the weapon. He handled it by the trigger guard, and sniffed at the muzzle. It had been fired all right, and quite recently. His match revealed pearl-handled butt plates and that meant there ought to be a good chance of tracing the weapon. Very likely it was one of a pair.

Ed changed his grip on it, testing the balance of it. The gun felt good. For a time, he stood quite still, aiming it at one tree and then another. He then examined the cylinder and found that three shots had been fired. He felt sure that he was holding the murder weapon.

Moreover, it was one of the latest model Colts and he had seen a pair like this only a short while ago. Dan Lawrence! The young lawyer had received such a pair from his mother. They had been sent through the post to his law school when it was learned that he had qualified. Previously, they had belonged to his father, now deceased.

But if it was Dan's then it should have been on the table in the Old Barn. How then had it got to be where he found it?

His mind was seething with conjecture as he retraced his steps and went uphill, towards the body.

* * *

Hector Morissey, attorney-at-law, was a tall, broad-shouldered forty-year-old, with a forked fair moustache and a lot of hair at the nape of his neck and in his sideburns. He was standing with his hands on his hips in his black business suit and grey stetson. Skinner Kopak's body lay beneath his feet.

The lawyer turned sharply when he heard footsteps behind him. His hand went to the gun strapped to his waist, but he arrested its progress when he recognised the familiar profile.

He remarked: '*You*, Ed? How come you are down in an area usually given over to courtin' couples?'

His glance went to the gun which Ed was carrying, and the weapon changed hands.

'I might ask you the same thing, brother. But in any case, I'm only twenty-eight. Not too old, I hope, to be interested in pretty girls.' His tone changed as he sensed the bleak look in his brother's eyes. 'I came alone, drawn by the sounds of gunfire, as I was returning to the Old Barn from the other end of town. That appears to be the murder weapon. It should be easy to identify.'

While the lawyer looked over the weapon, a heavily built man came down the path and took up a position alongside of the lawyer. He was breathing hard. This was Richard Speed, the town marshal. He had hollow cheeks, a big jaw and a brown bushy moustache through which he was breathing. Speed always looked the same, in his high-crowned brown stetson, his faded check-patterned shirt and black leather vest.

The lawyer said: 'Ed, here, was down before us. He found what appears to be the murder weapon somewhere lower down. How do you like the look of it?'

Dick Speed took the revolver and handled it gingerly. He whistled soundlessly as he saw the finish on it and the expensive butt plates. Already, he was trying over in his mind an owner for the weapon. The lawyer interrupted his deliberations with an obvious question.

'Eh? Oh, no. Hal Renton wasn't anywhere about. I sent a messenger along to his house to tell him we had a corpse for him. He turns in early, but, for an undertaker of his age he can turn out real fast. He won't be long.'

In the few minutes which elapsed before the appearance of the black moustached undertaker, Ed told all he had found and heard, and tentatively confirmed that the murder weapon might be one of the pair belonging to Dan Lawrence.

Marshal Speed held a match above Kopak's face and chest while the undertaker gave the body a cursory examination. While his eyes were busy, the undertaker's hands were hastily pushing his shirt tail inside his trousers.

He started to talk rather breathlessly. 'Hm, I don't figure many folks will take time out to mourn *this* fellow's loss, marshal. A couple of my men will be along in a minute. I don't figure we ought to haul the old Doc out of bed at this hour. Daylight will do for the examination, won't it?'

Marius Wood, the ancient town doctor, was in his seventy-sixth year; a tall, spindly man whose dark everyday clothes hung on his shrunken frame as though they had been intended for a much slimmer man. He followed his practice seven days a week, but he made it known to all and sundry that unnecessary night work ruined him for the chores of the following day.

Speed said: 'Sure, Hal, get him up to your place an' leave the medical examination for tomorrow. Heck an' me, we have a little business to do. We'll see you later.'

Marshal and lawyer went back up the path, closely followed by Ed. It soon became clear that he was going to accompany them on any initial investigation, and neither of them had any inclination to send him away. They knew the quality of his brains, and besides, he had been the first investigator on the scene. The trio headed first for the dance hall, where the marshal announced that he would like all who still remained to stay put for a few minutes while he had a chance to ask a few questions.

Before ending his short speech, he let

it be known that Skinner Kopak was the man lying dead, and with that the whole of the crowd remained stunned for a while, giving him a chance to give them a close scrutiny.

Obviously, there were several young couples in the place who had been out to the creek together, but they had now separated and had sought the company of their kin.

Ed ascertained that the Winders had driven off shortly before the shooting. The old couple had Pearl with them, and Dan had not been back to collect his weapons or his hat. Most of the weapons had been collected from the table. Two or three men were on benches, or seated in chairs, sleeping off an excess of punch. Their guns were on the table. Dan Lawrence's belt and holsters were there and easily identifiable, but one of the holsters was empty.

Speed pushed the murder gun into the empty holster and found that it fitted there quite snugly. The Morissey brothers were among those who witnessed the brief experiment. For a time, the peace officer was not at all sure what he ought to do next.

Various small groups came up to him and asked permission to leave. He asked questions as they came to his mind, but all were permitted to leave and warned that they might be questioned later.

Oddly enough, Hector Morissey, who was usually bursting with questions on such an occasion, was noticeably silent. The lawyer, who had taken on young Dan Lawrence just a few short weeks earlier, had a lot to think about.

Very soon, the building was empty. The musicians left hard on the heels of the last of the dancers. That left the trio of investigators and Reg Yarby, the livery hand. The trio seemed to be hesitating over a course of action.

Yarby looked troubled. 'Gents, I'd hate to be the one to tell you your business. I saw what the marshal did with that murder weapon an' I'd agree it sure looks black for young Lawrence. But ain't you jumpin' to the conclusion that he's done the shootin' an' then vamoosed? Why, he might be lyin' down that slope near to death at this very minute. I figure the area ought to be searched again.'

Marshal Speed was quick to agree. He sent the livery hand off to the peace office to collect the deputy and the old jailor who slept in the office. Yarby took them instructions to quietly search the town for Lawrence. If he showed up, he was to be taken along to the peace office and held there.

The marshal, the lawyer and the detective went along to the hotel. There, they borrowed lanterns from the manager and collected two other men to help them in their search of the creekside area. This time the search lasted for upwards of two hours, but the courting spot had no more secrets to give up.

★ ★ ★

Reg Yarby was a light sleeper. In the past ten years he had never stayed on his bed for more than five or six hours. In searching the town for young Lawrence he had subjected his suspect back to a rather cutting breeze, and, as a result of the pain which it had engendered, he was on his feet again the next morning by just after seven. He heated up coffee in the small office which was his headquarters, and brought in buckets of water from the pump at the rear. He was swishing away with a worn-down broom at the cobbled floor when an unaccountable sensation made his neck hairs prickle.

He had the feeling that he was observed, and yet he could not be sure of it. After one of the seemingly longest minutes of his life, his attention was taken by a movement and a sound coming from the loft. He looked up and saw to his amazement that someone had spent the night in the hay.

Dan Lawrence was sitting up there with short lengths of hay sticking out of his formidable red hair. Very slowly, Dan stood up and reached out for the top of the ladder which stood against the loft. The smell of horses appeared to be nauseating him.

'Good — good mornin', Reg. I — I don't figure I asked your permission to come up here last night. The fact is, I can't even remember comin' in. Maybe I ought to sit down a while longer till my legs feel a bit steadier. Did you see me come in?'

Yarby slowly shook his head. He pulled a chew of tobacco out of his overall pocket and nibbled the end of it. 'Take your time, by all means, Dan, 'cause you'll need to be steady an' to have a clear head when you're ready to go. Don't mind me, I've got a job of work to do.'

Dan nodded, smiled briefly and sat down again, massaging his head and then gingerly feeling over his stomach. He knew that he had been unwise in the amount of that potent punch which he had consumed the night before. He groped around for details of what had happened directly prior to his arriving at the livery, but no thoughts would come. Meanwhile, Reg Yarby worked away with his broom and pail and whistled incessantly.

From time to time, the stable hand cocked an interested eye in the direction of the loft. He did not hurry the young man, however, and he made no sort of move to send word to the peace office that Dan had been found. Whatever had to be done would be done as soon as the young galoot was feeling a little steadier.

Eventually, Dan came down the ladder and thankfully accepted a mug of coffee. Although it was hot, he drank it down rather quickly and then held his stomach as though the sudden arrival of the hot liquid was about to make him vomit.

Reg shook his head. 'Dan, boy, you sure ain't wise in small things.'

'What? What was that, Reg?'

The older man shook his head. 'As

soon as you feel fit to make a move you are to go along to the marshal's office and speak to him. He'll have questions to ask you, an' make sure you go straight there. Understand?'

Wonderingly, Dan nodded. He had a feeling that something very bad had happened in the time after the punch had robbed him of his senses. Peace office talk had to be serious. So he tried really hard to clear his thoughts and presently, he stepped out of doors and walked up the street.

Dick Speed was in the office on his own. His staff had gone down the street to take breakfast. He acted kind of surprised when Dan walked in with his hair still tousled, but he gestured for him to take an upright chair on the visitors' side of the desk. Dan sat on the very edge and looked far from comfortable.

'I've been sleepin' in the loft at the livery. Reg said for me to come along here straight away and talk to you. What is it you want, marshal?'

'You really have no idea, Dan?'

The youngster shook his head. Speed pointed to the pearl-handled weapon lying on his desk. He said: 'While you were out of the dance hall last night, Skinner Kopak was shot to death down by the creek with this gun. It happens to be yours, I think. Now, did you see Skinner when you were out with Pearl?'

Dan slowly rose to his feet, his normally fresh-complexioned face turning pale. He wanted to ask Speed to repeat what he had said, but he knew that he had heard it right and that there was no call to have it repeated.

'I didn't see Skinner at all yesterday, marshal. But I can see that I'll have lots of questions to answer when my head gets clearer. How would it be if I stretched out in a cell till my hangover wears off? That way, you know where I am, an' I do myself a favour by stretching out in a quiet place.'

Speed thought over this suggestion. He pondered for a long time.

'All right, Dan, we'll do that. You get

into that first cell and sleep yourself sober. Meantime, I'll turn the key an' mosey out to make a few more enquiries.'

Dan entered the cell indicated and stretched out on his back on the wooden bench. As the marshal stepped close to lock the door, he noted that his prisoner's expression looked troubled and hopeless.

3

At a little after ten o'clock the following morning, Hector Morissey called in at his office after making two or three calls in the centre of the town. He talked with his elderly male clerk, gave a few instructions, explained where he was going and left the building again with a small cigar between his lips.

His steps were slow and measured. He crossed the fronts of three buildings and slowed down even more when he came to the double-fronted edifice which had a shop and an office opening onto the sidewalk. The shop was that belonging to Skinner Kopak, and as might be expected it was still closed. The door of the office next door was ajar. A legend painted on the upper half of the window suggested that the tenant was a private investigator. The lawyer was calling to talk with his detective brother.

He tapped briefly on the door and stepped into the small square-shaped office. Ed was sitting in a swivel chair with his booted legs up on the scarred desk top. A single filing cabinet in a far corner was closed and had dust on it. An old newspaper was lying folded on the visitor's chair. A thin column of smoke was spiralling up from the brown paper cigarette in the corner of Ed's mouth.

The detective turned sharply, saw who was visiting him and promptly turned his head away again, apparently contemplating deeply over his private thoughts. Hector walked round the desk, cleaned off the upright chair with the newspaper, and sat down facing his brother.

'Good morning, Ed. Have you heard the latest developments?'

Ed rolled the cigarette around his mouth before he answered.

'Good morning, brother. I talked

with Reg Yarby. Your junior pardner has turned up. He's in custody. I reckon you must have been visitin' him.'

'I did call in to talk to Marshal Dick Speed, but I didn't get the chance to speak to Dan because he was snorin' loudly in the cell. Frankly, Ed, I'm worried about young Lawrence. If he was really drunk on that punch he might have done anything. This far we haven't raised much evidence which suggests that he didn't do the shootin' last night. What do you think?'

Ed shrugged. 'Like all good detectives I have an open mind. I reckon that if you dig around for a while you'll come up with a few useful pointers. You'll soon know whether or not you made a wise choice in takin' on Dan Lawrence as a junior pardner.'

Hector tugged at his ear lobe. His relationship with his brother had been anything but a smooth one since Ed had given up his legal training for the uneasy profession of private investigator. He wondered just how much interest Ed had in Lawrence and the law firm's problems.

'Talkin' of diggin' around, Ed. I kind of thought you'd like to do any preliminary investigating necessary. We shall not know for sure whether Dan has a charge to face until Walter McGurk, the county attorney, comes over from the county seat. But Walter is a great one for prosecuting. If Dan faces a murder charge I shall have to act in his defence. And then I could pay you a retainer while you rake up evidence useful to the defence.'

Ed had listened calmly this far. Now, he lowered his feet to the floor and wagged a speculate finger in Heck's direction.

'Now, see here, brother, if you want to retain me do the job officially, then I'll do the diggin' around for you. Otherwise, you have no right to be askin' me. I have other things to do with my time. Besides, I haven't any special interest in Dan Lawrence. If you want my opinion, the fellow is a fool.'

Maddeningly, Ed reached across the desk and grabbed the ancient newspaper, which he pretended to read. The lawyer coloured up beyond it, but he had no intention of losing his temper.

Hector said: 'Now see here, Ed, you can't pretend you're not interested in this case, because I know you are. I can't retain you yet for the reason I've already given, but I really think you ought to be making a few enquiries, though. After all, you haven't any other business on, an' it must be nearly ten days since you cleared up your last case, that theft at the hotel. So why not go along with the case for a while, let the local folks see you're interested.'

Ed sniffed. He glanced at the clock on the wall, which was fast, and then shot Hector a bleak glance. 'Thank you for your interest, brother, but I never make a practice of workin' for nothing. Be kind enough to close the door on the way out.'

The lawyer rose to his feet, glowered at him and stalked out, slamming the door behind him. Ed smiled rather grimly as he watched his brother walk away through the window. Very soon, however, the smile faded, and his thoughts went back to Dan Lawrence and then to Pearl Winder. He brooded over the obvious interest which Pearl had shown to the young lawyer the night before.

He began to exercise his mind on theories about the crime, building into them the few facts which he knew.

★　★　★

In spite of the way in which he had answered his brother that morning, Ed had joined Marshal Speed in the early afternoon when the peace officer had called on him and intimated that he was about to ride out to the Winder spread.

Around two o'clock they walked their mounts through the paddock gate of the horse ranch west of town and only paused when they were at the hitch rail under the gallery of the main building.

41

Dave Winder, Pearl's father, was sitting in a wicker chair, his big hat pushed back off his forehead and a broad belt supporting his ample paunch.

He emptied and put down a glass of fruit juice, before giving his attention to the two newcomers. The peace officer received a smile, and Ed just a curt nod.

'Come on up, won't you? I guess it must be right that young Lawrence is in some way connected with the shooting we heard as we left town last night. You come to talk to me about it, marshal?'

Speed stepped over a litter of saddlery and sat down, clearing another seat for Ed at the same time.

'Good day to you, Dave. It's good of you to take time out to talk to us, but it is really Pearl we have to talk to. When a murder is committed we have to talk to a whole lot of people. Sometimes it ain't really convenient, but I can't rightly help it, though. Perhaps you'd be good enough to ask the girl to step through this way for a few minutes?'

The old rancher did not seem any too pleased, but he nodded after a pause, and stepped inside his front door to make his wants known.

'Mabel, I want you to have Pearl step through to the front gallery for a few minutes. We have the marshal here. He wants to ask her a few questions. You hear me?'

'I hear you husband,' a faint voice said from the back of the house, and presently Pearl came through, looking mildly embarrassed at being seen in a pair of denims and a man's shirt which showed off her figure to advantage.

There were twin spots of high colour in her cheeks as she smiled briefly and shyly at each of the visitors and then obeyed her father's instructions to sit down and listen to the questions. While she was settling down, Mabel Winder, the mother, came through from the back of the house. She was a tight-lipped woman in a coarse working dress. Her grey hair was trimmed short. She was nervously wiping her hands on

43

a soiled apron. Prompted by her husband, she asked the visitors what they would like to drink. Both decided upon coffee, and she withdrew to get it.

Dick Speed briefly touched his hat, and began. 'Pearl, Skinner Kopak was killed down beside the creek last night. Now, as you were there for a while with Dan Lawrence, I have to ask you to tell us what happened when you were away from the Old Barn.'

The girl blushed, glanced shyly at Ed and then looked away again. Dave Winder, a brusque man at the best of times, did not take kindly to questioning of this nature and he said as much, making the marshal bite his lip with annoyance. Ed Morissey, who had little to lose, saw that as his opportunity to talk.

'Pearl, Dan's gun was the one used to kill Kopak, so you'll see how important it is that you answer the marshal's question. We have to know a whole lot more about what Dan did last night, after the two of you went out.'

44

'Well, Ed, if Pa thinks it's all right to tell you.' The girl glanced at her father and received grudging approval. She went on: 'It's all kind of embarrassin', gents. You see, Dan walked down the path with me. We were arm in arm. He was sayin' that the sound of the water made him feel romantic. He, er, he might have kissed me on the way down. But, well, when we got there. To the path alongside of the creek, that is, the walkin' up and down seemed to make him feel giddy.

'He complained that his stomach was playin' him up. I asked him how that was, an' he must have been feelin' real bad because he was impatient with me. He pushed me down in the grass, told me to stay there for a moment and plunged towards the water. I think he was lyin' down with his head over the creek. I — I heard certain noises.'

Pearl appeared to dry up. Her father was the one to start her off again.

'You mean the young jasper was drunk an' he started to throw up!

Wasn't that so? Well, answer the question! Somebody had to ask it!'

'I guess that was so, Pa. Dan must have vomited. I felt angry with him at first, an' then he came back to me an' I could tell by his face that he was feelin' real bad. He looked an awful odd colour. So when he asked me to make my own way back to the Barn I decided to humour him. I went back, and that was that. Ma was showin' a little tiredness, so Pa suggested we start for home without delay.

'We were actually on the way out of town when we heard the gun shots, so we didn't really know what had happened until a man came out from town this morning with a message.'

At this moment there was a brief break in the discussion while Mrs. Winder delivered the drinks. The two visitors were both thinking that Dave Winder showed a singular lack of curiosity in not finding out more about the firing before driving on to his ranch.

Having seen that the coffee was to

the guests' satisfaction, Mabel Winder savoured the atmosphere on the gallery, decided that it was no place for her, and withdrew again, nervously pursing her thin lips.

'Was there anything else you wanted to ask the girl, marshal?' Winder asked rather bluntly.

Dick Speed felt sure that there was at least one important question he ought to have answered before he left the ranch, but for once his mind was not functioning. He turned and bestowed a questioning glance upon Ed Morissey.

Ed said quietly: 'The marshal wanted to ask you if Dan had one of his guns with him when you left the dance, Pearl.'

The girl nibbled her finger, as though surprised at the question. She started to shake her head, became aware that they wanted a spoken answer and then blurted it out.

'Oh, no, at least I don't think so. After all, a revolver is a pretty big weapon to carry. He didn't have any gun belt on. I think I must have known if he'd been carryin' one. It would have had to be stuck in the back of his waist belt, wouldn't it?'

Dick Speed nodded. The two visitors rose to their feet, as though suddenly keen to be on their way. Ed hurriedly emptied his coffee cup and moved towards the steps while the marshal offered his thanks for Dave Winder's co-operation.

Ed was seeing to the cinching of his buckskin when Pearl, who had mildly defied her father in not retiring into the house, appeared beside him. She stroked the white blaze on the animal's head.

She murmured: 'Ed, surely the marshal doesn't think that Dan shot Skinner Kopak. Does he? Do you believe it?'

Obviously, Pearl was concerned about Dan and his predicament. Ed wished that she had been worrying over him, instead. But he would not have cared to be in Dan's position over the shooting.

He tried to sound impartial when he answered.

'I don't think the marshal believes Dan did it. But someone did, and he has to find out the truth. Right now, he's askin' around, an' tryin' to keep an open mind. Dan was in the lock-up when we left town, but he volunteered to go in the cell while the enquiries were goin' on, because he didn't feel very well this morning.'

Mr. Winder was making impatient noises up on the gallery, but Pearl stayed alongside of Ed for a few moments more. 'I do hope the marshal finds out who did the shooting without any long delay, Ed. For Dan's sake. He won't like bein' in a cell at all, especially since he's a qualified lawyer.'

Ed could have retorted that any man, whatever his calling in life, tended to dislike a period in a cell. But he kept such thoughts to himself.

'I don't think he's taken much harm yet. The uncertainty about the shooting and his own lapse of memory will probably ensure that he doesn't drink as much punch the next time he goes to a dance, though. Anyway, he's not your problem, unless you want it that way. Remember there are plenty of capable and eligible young men in town beside him.'

'Why, Ed! How can you talk that way? You really must be jealous of Dan. But please go on helpin' the marshal to find out the truth.'

Ed nodded and mounted up, while the girl turned away and ran back into the house. Dave Winder stood on his gallery watching them until they were through the paddock gate. He then followed his daughter indoors.

On the way back, Ed asked if Mervin Hayes knew about Dan's incarceration. Speed gave him a rather strange look.

'Sure, he'll know now. His foreman was in town this morning, an' he took the tidings back to the ranch. But I don't think Mervin is particularly keen on his wife's grown up son. It's the mother who will be distressed, of course.'

Following another brief interval, Ed asked another question. 'Uppermost in most folks' minds is who did it, Dick. Do you think Dan could have done the killin'?'

Speed scowled so that his hollow cheeks and large jaw seemed more exaggerated. 'Of course he could have done it. We don't know, do we? I happen to know he had a quarrel with Skinner, though, when he'd only been back in town for three or four days.'

'But you are not suggestin' that Dan committed a premeditated murder, are you, Dick? After all, about three young men of the town have had words with Skinner over his peeping activities, to my knowledge, and there might have been more. If you don't come up with something definite soon, you'll have to let Dan loose.'

Speed knew this, but he felt that he had done something in the eyes of the townsfolk in locking up the young man, even temporarily.

He sounded brusque when he answered. 'For the present Dan stays where he is. His future will depend to a great extent upon the deliberations of the county attorney.'

After that, they rode on in silence. Ed, for his part, had a premonition that Walter McGurk would try to build a case against the young prisoner.

4

Walter D. McGurk, the county attorney, was an imposing figure at any hour of the day. In his late forties, his black goatee beard, his brown tailored suit and round black hat marked him down as a person of some importance. His straight-backed, almost military, way of walking appeared to offset his lack of inches.

At ten o'clock in the morning he left the office in Silver Creek of the town marshal and set off along the boards in the direction of Hector Morissey's establishment. When he had gone a few yards, Speed, the town marshal, stepped out of his office doorway and stood watching the attorney as he moved off up the street.

Speed had never come across him before, and the way in which he had gone into the evidence in the Kopak case had been something of a revelation to him. The directness of the attorney's gaze had made Dan Lawrence shudder in his cell.

McGurk liked to impress new people with his directness and his general air of aggression. Those who had faced him in court knew him for a very determined man who seldom ever deviated from the course which he had worked out for his case.

Heck Morissey's clerk almost sprang to attention when McGurk appeared in the outer office.

'Mr. McGurk? Mr. Morissey is expecting you, if you'd be so kind as to go straight in, sir.'

McGurk nodded, at once lost interest in the fellow, and stepped through the small swinging gate and then on into the private office. Morissey was seated behind a big padded desk with an array of papers around him.

'Good-day to you, McGurk. Take a seat.'

Morissey finished writing on a

document, put aside his pen, and sat back, making a steeple of the fingers of his two hands.

'Don't tell me. Let me guess. You think there's sufficient evidence against Lawrence for him to stand trial for the murder of Kopak. Is that your conclusion?'

McGurk, an American of Irish descent, grinned briefly. 'That's about the size of things. It's good for the county attorney to be quick to prosecute. You know my theories in these matters, Morissey. I suppose that, seeing the young man is a new addition to your firm, you'll be defending him?'

'I'd never live it down if I didn't defend him, Walter. All the same, I'm surprised you think there's a case to answer. Now, let me see, the circuit judge won't be presiding in the county seat for another two or three weeks. That's a fairly long wait for a young man like Lawrence. Will you agree to his being set free in the meantime?'

McGurk tugged at his chin beard,

but he had already thought over this possible development, and his mind was made up. 'It's always a bit risky, letting people go before the trial, but, well, if his legal next of kin will sign an appearance bond I don't see why he shouldn't have his liberty. After all, you'll be able to keep an eye on him. I suppose he'll be back workin' for you as soon as he is released?'

Morissey nodded. 'I certainly hope so, Walter. By the way, if the bond is forfeit, how much will the fine be?'

McGurk grinned for the second time. 'I always believe in a goodly round sum, Hector, as you know. The figure will be ten thousand dollars. I understand that the family has a ranch in these parts. They'll be able to raise it, I dare say.'

Morissey frowned, furrowing his brow. 'The present rancher is the prisoner's stepfather. Moreover, he has a reputation these days for being tight-fisted.'

McGurk did not seem interested any more. He was getting to his feet when he replied. 'Jest so long as a man of substance signs the bond you can have Lawrence out of the cell. My office will keep you informed of any details, developments. If I don't see you before, we'll meet in the county court when the case comes up. I'll say so long for now, an' wish you well in your preparations for the defence.'

On the way he paused and looked back. 'It looks as if you've picked yourself a darned fine assistant this time, Heck!'

'Don't count your chickens about gettin' a conviction this time, Walter!' Morissey retorted.

The clerk, who had heard and witnessed the cross-talk, watched his master walk back into the private office and thought he looked troubled in spite of his words.

* * *

Ed Morissey was one of perhaps two dozen townsmen who attended the funeral that afternoon of Skinner Kopak. No new jobs of work had turned up for the young detective, and he was more than a little curious to know whether anyone from out of town would turn up for the burial.

He had half expected a surprise visitor or two, but on this occasion he was disappointed. No one, other than the obvious townsmen and dignitaries, turned up to mark the occasion. And those who did go to Boot Hill were quick to disperse when the parson had said his piece and the ceremony was over.

Ed was not particularly keen to be interviewed by his brother, but curiosity about the possible developments in the case against Dan Lawrence made him slow his steps when the people were coming away.

Hector was slow to detach himself from the doctor and the undertaker, but when he had done so he hurried after his younger brother and caught him up on the outskirts of town.

'Ed, may I ask a question without seeming rude?'

'Go ahead and try, brother. What is it you want to know?'

'Have you had any other work in since we talked last?'

Ed favoured the lawyer with a wry smile. Instead of answering outright in the negative, he posed another question. 'All right, Heck, what is it you want me to do?'

The lawyer began to relax a little. 'I can tell you that there is a case against Dan Lawrence. The county attorney is determined to go ahead with the prosecution. But the case won't be handled in the county seat for two or three weeks. In the meantime, Dan Lawrence will want to be at liberty. I wondered if you could find time to ride out to the Diamond L this afternoon to talk with Mervin Hayes?'

Ed kicked a small stone out of his path. He waited until it came to rest some ten yards away before answering. 'If you are askin' like that, it don't sound as if I'm to be retained and paid. And, another thing, Mervin Hayes ain't the easiest man to interview. I hope what you want me to talk to him about doesn't have anything to do with money.'

Hector tugged at his ear lobe. They both stood aside while the doctor's buckboard went by. 'In an indirect way it has to do with money, Ed. You see, someone has to sign an appearance bond to ensure that Dan turns up for his trial. If Dan *did* happen to skip the trial the person who signed the bond would have to forfeit ten thousand dollars.'

Ed whistled, long and deliberately.

'Not that Dan is likely to be missin' when the time comes,' the lawyer added hastily.

They discussed the proposed journey for another five minutes, took a drink together, and then parted.

* * *

Mrs. Mary Hayes, who had been previously Mrs. Mary Lawrence, was a small dumpy woman of forty-five with a well-rounded figure. She was fresh complexioned, with short greying brown hair. The colour in her face suggested high blood pressure.

Late in the afternoon Ed found the woman sitting in a swinging hammock-style seat on the front gallery of the Diamond L. Along with a Mexican woman servant she had just completed the washing of many sheets and blankets, which were now hanging on a long clothes line at the rear of the building.

As the rider came across the last patch of ground before the house the woman shaded her eyes, stared hard at him, and then stood up, smiling broadly.

'Why, Ed, how nice of you to ride out this way. I think you must have brought some news about my poor boy. Is he takin' it very badly, spendin' all that time in the cell? I can't think how anybody who knows Dan could think that he'd shoot a fellow like Skinner

Kopak. It's all a mystery to me.'

Ed said he thought Dan was taking his spell in the cell as well as could be expected. He dismounted, hitched the buckskin to the rail, and clambered up onto the gallery, lifting his hat and pulling forward an upright chair so that he could join the woman.

As he sat down he found himself reflecting that he liked the former Mrs. Mary Lawrence a whole lot more than her red-headed offspring.

'I've been wantin' to ride into town ever since they put Dan away,' the woman went on, 'but my husband, Mervin, is a hard-headed fellow. He's not at all keen for me to present myself at the peace office for a visitin' session. I wish I knew what to do for the best. But perhaps I'll know better when you've given me the latest news.'

Ed thought Mrs. Hayes deserved a few crumbs of comfort, so he talked nicely to her. 'If you are at all interested, Mrs. Hayes, I don't think your son shot Skinner Kopak. But two things, probably, stand against him at the moment. The first is that the gun used belonged to Dan, and the second is that he parted from the girl he was with, Pearl Winder, and did not show up again until the next morning. The punch he drank was rather strong and, consequently, he has difficulty in remembering some of the details of what happened that night.'

Mrs. Hayes nodded, looked away, and trapped a few tears in her handkerchief. 'Did, did your brother, the lawyer, send you here, Ed?'

'He did, indeed, Mrs. Hayes. I came to talk with your husband about doing the necessary for getting Dan out of the cell.'

The woman brightened at once. Ed's words had put new heart into her. 'My husband is checking stock on home range, but he may not be back for a while. It's good to hear that Dan will be coming out soon, though. Your visit has done me good, Ed.'

Ed put a light to a smoke. 'He will

have to face the charge of havin' shot Skinner, Mrs. Hayes, but he can come out before the trial provided someone signs an appearance bond. There's a money risk involved in the event that Dan didn't turn up for the case at the county court. Do you think your husband will be willin' to sign the bond?'

Mary Hayes' face clouded. 'I wish I knew,' she answered, her voice scarcely above a whisper. 'He's so unpredictable.'

Fifteen minutes later the Mexican woman hurried out of the house with all the necessary utensils for coffee making. Ed wondered when she had received her instructions as his hostess had not moved from her seat to make contact with anyone.

Within minutes it became clear that the servant had seen signs of the master's return from home range. Mervin Hayes and four other riders came through the buildings and split up. Hayes came on alone to the house.

He frowned when he saw that there was a visitor.

His wife pushed him into the seat she had been occupying and, while he drank his coffee, stony-eyed, she recounted everything which had transpired between Ed and herself prior to his return.

Hayes was thirsty, and slow to answer. He spoke with slow deliberation. 'Morissey, you can tell that lawyer brother of yours that I paid a lot of money for my wife's son to be properly trained in law school. But, after that, I stopped being a charitable institution. I don't pay out any more for him. This appearance bond you spoke of. How much money is involved if he doesn't turn up when he's wanted?'

Ed looked the rancher over. With his small hooked nose and turned-down mouth he looked what he was, a tough, self-reliant, self-made man who had little time for the weaknesses of others.

'The amount is ten thousand dollars, Mr. Hayes.'

Hayes blinked hard, but soon got

over his surprise. 'You've come to the wrong man, Mr. Morissey. Tell your brother my stepson is of age. And since he took up with the law office he is the attorney's responsibility. I ain't signin' anything to get him out of that cell, an' that's final.'

Hayes stamped indoors. His wife dissolved into a flood of tears. Ed reluctantly began to prepare for his departure. Hayes' reaction to the request had not surprised him in the least. Ed had just mounted up and was touching his hat to Mrs. Hayes when the rancher came out of doors again with a towel in his hand.

'Hold on a minute, Morissey! My wife wants to visit her son in town. I'd take it as a favour if you'd escort her there!'

Hayes gave orders to his hands to run out the buckboard. They moved hurriedly to do his bidding. With a slight show of reluctance, Ed dismounted again. He waited while Mrs. Hayes went indoors and made her brief preparations.

5

Ed was late getting to sleep that night. In spite of a feeling of jealousy when Pearl was in his thoughts, he could now manage to feel sorry for the young man in the cell. He knew that Dan's father had died at a time when the youngster needed him, and that Mrs. Lawrence had been forced to marry again because she was in a bad way financially.

Poor Dan. His mother was the only person with any real feeling for him, and she was obviously without cash these days and altogether under the thumb of her domineering second husband.

The following morning Ed still did not have any other business to occupy his thoughts. His funds were beginning to run low. He hoped that they would not get so low that he would have to take a temporary job of some sort or another to keep body and soul together. If only Hector would offer him a few dollars to help with the defence of the Lawrence boy!

Heck was slow to make an offer, and that was probably because he would have to pay for Dan's defence out of his own pocket. Hayes would claim that he had given no instructions to Heck and that he, therefore, was paying no bills.

After dawdling for a long time over his breakfast, Ed saw Speed's deputy go past the eating house, and that started him thinking about the occupied cell all over again. He made up his mind quite suddenly to go along to the office and talk with the prisoner. There would be no difficulty about getting to talk to Dan because just about all the town knew that Ed had been working with the marshal in the early stages of the investigation.

The jailor, Limpy Cord, was the only officer inside the office when Ed went in. The old man was stripped down to his under vest, mopping the floor and blowing out his flowing white moustache as he worked. He turned and looked a little disgusted when he saw that Ed meant to stay.

'Limpy, I want to talk to young Dan, but I won't get in your way. That I promise you.'

'Hell an' tarnation, Ed, you sure do pick the darnedest times to do your visitin'. Jest when I'm in the thick of swabbin' out. I'll have to ask you to spread the paper over the floor and keep well to that side while I finish off!'

Dan got up off his wooden bench and looked relieved to see someone who wanted to talk to him. Ed was quick to pick up an old newspaper and use it in the way Limpy suggested. Soon he was standing on a paper oasis just outside the bars of the cell.

Dan said, rather sheepishly: 'Howdy, Ed, it's too much to expect that you've come along here with an order to set me free. How are you? How's your brother?'

'Take it easy, Dan,' Ed suggested.

'Heck does all right. You had your mother in here yesterday evening. That must have been unsettling for you. She will have told you that I was out to the ranch to try an' get your stepfather to sign an appearance bond. Mervin didn't want to know about it. And here you are, still locked up. Most folks in town don't believe you shot Skinner, and hardly anybody blames you even if you did. I wish I could do something to spring you out of jail, but it ain't easy. Not since that Irish county attorney came over here to set up a case against you. Do you have any ideas?'

'According to what Ma was sayin' it's a matter of finding someone who is willing to risk ten thousand dollars on whether I show up for my trial. We're supposed to have plenty of friends in an' around the town, an', anyway, the risk ain't all that great.

'My future lies with your brother's law firm. I'm not likely to make off and ruin my own chances of a good start in my chosen profession.'

Limpy paused in his swabbing, wheezing a little with the exertion, but neither of the two men in the office wanted to talk to him just at that moment. Dan flexed his fingers round the bars and looked embarrassed.

'I have an idea, but I don't know how good it is.'

'Go ahead, tell me about it,' Ed prompted.

'Well, I'm thinkin' about your brother. He's been in practice for quite some time now and some of his cases have paid off handsomely. I was wondering. Do you think he might have enough money in the bank to sign the appearance bond himself?'

Ed's sun-bleached eyebrows climbed his forehead. This suggestion had set him thinking. Hector was still a bachelor, but rumour had it that he was specially interested in a lady who lived in Placerville, the county seat. The lawyer kept his thoughts on matrimony to himself, but everybody in town knew how he had had men building a nice two-storey house with a garden for him in the best residential part of the town. He had only recently moved into the house. The point was, had he ploughed all his savings into it, or had he a sizeable nest egg set aside for purposes of matrimony?

Ed started to smile without being aware of it.

He said: 'I'll ask Heck about it, but don't build up your hopes too much, because I have no idea of the outcome. I don't know if he saves money, or whether he has spent all his earnings. I'll see what he says. And now, I think I'd better be going, Dan. Is there anything special you'd like sent in?'

Dan shook his head. 'Jest bring me hope of some sort. Shucks, Ed, it's my twenty-third birthday tomorrow. I don't want to celebrate it here in this cell!'

Ed shook the young prisoner by the hand and left rather hurriedly. Limpy eyed the door speculatively after he had gone, and slowly resumed his chores.

★ ★ ★

In the law office, half an hour later, Ed began his assault upon his brother. He talked carefully, using his hands expressively.

'In the circumstances, Heck, I believe you have only one course of action. You'll have to sign the paper yourself!'

The lawyer looked thoroughly taken aback. His mouth gaped, a thing which he scarcely ever allowed to happen. The older man closed his mouth in a grim line and looked pained.

He argued: 'What makes you think *I* have ten thousand dollars to take a chance on?' Ed failed to answer. In a slightly calmer tone Hector resumed. 'It is expectin' too much for the defending attorney to have to risk his own money to keep the client out of a cell for a few weeks. If the worst comes to the worst he'll have to stay in there. It — it'll strengthen his character. He'll never go off the straight and narrow after this.'

Ed traced a figure eight of smoke

through the air with his cigarette. He was studying the smoke when he went on. 'But these are special circumstances, seein' as how the client is a member of your own firm, Hector. Besides, he's quite repentant over everything that's happened. He'll come right back here an' start work, to your orders. As he says, his future lies right here. He wouldn't do anything to jeopardise his future.'

Hector brought out a cigar, as though it was his last, and carefully lit it. 'Nevertheless, it is still a risk, and members of my profession are trained to be cautious men.'

Ed acted as though he had suddenly become impatient. He rose to his feet and paced over to the door. 'If I were in his shoes I'd simply watch my chance and then bust out. Especially if it happened to be my birthday tomorrow.'

He nodded rather distantly and stepped out into the other office. He was perceptive enough to know from what had transpired that Hector had the necessary cash if he wanted to make the gesture. Maybe he would, when he had contemplated a little.

★ ★ ★

Dan Lawrence's birthday had progressed to the tenth hour when Hector Morissey strode importantly into the peace office and presented to Marshal Speed the signed appearance bond.

Dick Speed was exceedingly surprised. 'Is this what I think it is, Hector? Have you decided to take the risk yourself?'

The lawyer nodded and grinned. 'Dick, you are a better reader than your predecessor was. Sure, I want Dan out of that cell and I want him out right now.'

Beyond the bars the prisoner hooted with relief. The marshal and his jailor got some satisfaction over his joy. Limpy was the one to fetch the keys and open the door. Dan came out fast. He crossed to the street window, glanced through it as though he had never seen the thoroughfare before, and came back to await instructions from his liberator.

'Get yourself along to the office, Dan. I want a half day's work out of you. You can celebrate your birthday tonight. Let's go.'

* * *

By ten o'clock that evening the Silver Creek saloon was packed with men who knew about Dan Lawrence's liberation and his birthday. Some were merely there for a good time with a free drink or two thrown in, and others were really pleased to see the young fellow at liberty.

Dan had already consumed a useful quantity of beer and whiskey by the time the barman suggested he ought to issue his invitation to free drinks. The young man was quick to agree that the time was ripe. He climbed up on a tall stool and stood swaying upon it while the barman knocked for silence.

'Can you hear me, gents? You all know me, Dan Lawrence. I want you all to have a drink on me because it's my birthday an' it's good to be in this place instead of a cell. Jest move up to the bar an' tell the barman what you need. Tell him it's on me, he'll understand.'

There was a chorus of shouts of goodwill and thanks. Dan swayed and fell off the stool, but several pairs of hands caught him. He retrieved his pearl-handled six-gun, which had fallen to the floor. This was one of the pair. The other was still denied him as it had been retained for the court case which was pending. Dan held up the gun, and he beamed. All the worry of the past day or two seemed to have fallen from him. He whirled the gun around on his finger with the trigger guard.

Ed and Marshal Speed, who had just entered by the batwings, noticed the action on the part of Dan and exchanged glances. Each of them was just a little bit worried about him. They did not want to see him get into further trouble.

But Dan had the attention of everyone in the room. They cleared a space for him. Just beyond the end of the long bar there were two doors. Dan selected the first one for a bit of light-hearted target practice. He lined up his gun on the panels of the door and began to shoot. In the confined, smoky space, the gun shots were almost deafening, but the men put up with it.

He had fired sufficiently well with his first six bullets to have written a capital D in the door panel. While others called encouragement to him, he reloaded and repeated the performance. This time he shot out the shape of a letter L.

The room rocked with applause. It was well known that the owner did not like trick shooting in his saloon, but on this occasion he was nowhere to be seen. Ed and the marshal pushed through to Dan's side and moved up to the bar with him. They drank their free drinks slowly, observing him as they did so.

The amount he had drunk and the atmosphere in the building were making him sleepy. His talk was becoming slurred. Speed nodded to Ed and between them they headed for the door with him.

Dan protested, but they assured him that a sleep was what he needed more than anything else at that time. Some men shouted to Speed in a bantering tone, beseeching him not to lock Dan in a cell again. The marshal paused long enough to assure the drinkers that no such thing was likely to happen.

And then they were out in the fresh air, and Dan's legs had become rubbery. They got him as far as the law office building before he showed signs of recovery. The first thing his eyes clearly focussed on then was the lawyer's shingle over the door. He wanted to shoot a few decorative holes in it, but they dissuaded him, and presently they had laid him to sleep in his room above the offices.

He was snoring hard when they left him and went their respective ways. That night, another remarkable incident had occurred in the life of Dan Lawrence, but neither of these two had the slightest inkling about it. Had they known the consequences they would scarcely have been likely to sleep at all.

6

Tim Leeds, a slim lad of eighteen with curly black hair and a pointed chin, was the town's message runner. He also did odd jobs in various parts of town, such as office and saloon cleaning. Several years ago he had appeared in town on foot after running away from a wagon train heading further west.

One of Tim's regular jobs was that of cleaning the Silver Creek saloon. This he did every day of his life, and, as he did not particularly like the job, he never considered that the day had started until the chore was done.

On the morning after Dan Lawrence's party, Tim entered the saloon, as usual, between seven and eight in the morning and began to empty the spittoons and sprinkle sawdust on the floor. Ten minutes later he paused by the end of the bar to light up a half cigarette which he had kept behind his ear.

He frowned as the paper crackled and the smoke started to come through. The tobacco was strong and the taste was rather bitter. He was blinking his eyes and getting ready to move off again when he spotted a dark stain on the boards by the two doors.

The first door, into which Dan Lawrence had blasted his initials, was a broom cupboard. The other door led into a corridor which gave access to private rooms and to the rear. Hardly anyone ever went into the broom cupboard other than Tim. This was why he was so surprised to see the stain. So far as he knew he had not left anything in the cupboard which could have spilled over.

His feet were bare, as he had kicked off his mocassins to do the floor. Now he advancedly gingerly, reluctant to touch the stain with his feet. A small round splash, hitherto unnoticed, stuck to the sole of his foot. He frowned with annoyance and leaned over the main stain, gripping the door handle and pulling it open.

He had had a premonition that something was amiss, but the opening of the door took him completely by surprise. His mouth opened wide in a soundless cry of alarm as a crumpled man's body in soiled trail clothes folded forward and slipped to the ground in a grotesque position.

The fellow was dead, of course. The blood had dripped from his chest down the inside of the door and spread out in a large pool, seeping under it. As soon as Tim got over the worst of the shock, the faces of men in the town known to him went through his mind in a never-ending stream. Each time he visualised a face he tried to fit it to the crumpled body lying at his feet.

After a time he came to the conclusion that this man was a complete stranger. He got down on his knees, which were just covered by the ragged bottoms of his pants, and peered at the face of the fallen man from several angles.

The man had been ugly. His bloodshot eyes protruded. His face was fleshy and covered by one day's growth of brown stubble. Tim felt a kind of relief in not knowing him, but that did not last for long. Now, he had to think about what was to be done. He was bright enough to see that the fellow had been killed by accident when hiding in the cupboard the night before. Very probably Dan Lawrence's bullets had killed him when the initials had been put into the door.

Having come to this conclusion, the youth moved away from the corpse and stuck his elbows up on the counter, propping his head on them. An array of bottles faced him behind the bar. If he had been a drinking man this would have been a good time to take a shot, but alcohol had no hold on him.

Dan Lawrence was a man much observed by Tim, and also looked up to. Dan was getting the sort of start in the town which Tim would have liked for himself. Tim felt he had to help Dan, if he possibly could, in the matter of this dead man. He had no idea how Dan would react to what had happened, but he ought to be told without delay.

Tim came to a decision. He slipped into his mocassins and grabbed his straw hat and ran off up the street. His speeding figure was a commonplace sight in the town, so no one who saw him attached any special significance to it.

He ran until he came to the alley beside the lawyer's office, and did not pause until he was at the top of the outside staircase which led to the quarters above. After glancing around him to see if he was observed, he knocked on the glass panel in the door and waited.

After a second knock, Dan called out rather hoarsely to ask who it was and for the visitor to step inside. Tim did so, and a few seconds later Dan stepped out from behind a curtain in a crumpled dressing-gown and demanded to know what Tim wanted at that time of the day.

'Mr. Dan, there's something you ought to know about down at the saloon. You remember shooting your initials into that door last night?'

Dan's legs appeared to weaken. He still remembered all too clearly his spell in the cell. He fumbled sideways for a chair and sank into it rather hurriedly.

'Well, go on, Tim, don't keep me in suspense. What about last night? I got back here all right, didn't I? I seem to remember a couple of fellows bringin' me back shortly after the distribution of free drinks.'

Tim nodded sagely, his straw hat clasped to his rather thin chest. 'There was a man in the cupboard when you were shooting, Mr. Dan. Goodness knows what he was doin' in there. But your bullets, some of them, hit him in the chest. He died, an' he stayed in there till this morning, when I found him on account of the blood comin' under the door. So you see, I thought you ought to know. I'm tellin' you first, I mean.'

Dan's face looked haggard. He was thinking that he had only been out on a kind of parole for a few hours, and now another man had died, almost certainly this time from his gun. It was a dastardly thing to happen right on the heels of the Kopak setback. How did that alter things? he wondered. Another man dead by one of the Dan Lawrence pair of guns. How would it look in court when he had to face the hostile county attorney, Walter McGurk? The prosecutor would surely manage to mention what had happened in some way. He would introduce it into the case, even though the two incidents were not related, other than by accident.

He trembled to think what such revelations would have upon a jury of men who did not know him. His head was cleared now by the shock. He felt that his luck had finally run out. He was not likely now to practice as an attorney, at least not in this town. There would be repercussions over this latest catastrophe, however the ordinary towns-men saw it.

He felt that there was only one thing to do now. Clear out.

'Do you think anyone else will know about the man in the saloon yet? Who was he? You haven't mentioned his name.'

'I don't think anyone else will have seen him so far, Mr. Dan, because I'm the only person who goes into the saloon at this time of the morning. I don't know who he is, either. I looked at his face a lot, but I've never seen it before. He was a stranger, I think. Maybe somebody who wanted a free drink.'

Dan by this time was on his feet again, pacing up and down and breathing hard because of the tension which was building up in him. His fingers encountered a silver dollar in his pocket. He took it out and tossed it across to Tim, who caught it and pocketed it gratefully.

'Thanks for coming to me first, Tim. And there's something I want you to do for me. Go along to the livery an' ask to have my horse saddled and ready for the trail in ten minutes. Think you can do that without raisin' too much curiosity? I have to go away for a while.'

'I'll be glad to do what you say, Mr. Dan, an' I won't say why you have to go away. I know it was an accident, even if other people don't. I hope you'll be all right wherever you go. Adios.'

Dan went over and gripped the lad by the shoulder in a kindly fashion. He then went back to his sleeping alcove and started to dress rather hurriedly.

★   ★   ★

Thirty minutes later a bleary-eyed barman stumbled over the dead body and shocked himself out of a mild hangover. He picked himself up, poured out about three fingers of whiskey and tossed them down his throat before trotting off to the rear corridor in search of his master.

Horace Black, the saloon owner, came back into the main area with him and ran over to the spot on short thick legs. Black was a plump, hirsute man, a worrier. He looked his fifty years when he bent over the still figure, and started to perspire. His striped trousers were baggy at the knees and his buttoned vest was soiled with tobacco ash.

'Is he stiff? Has he been here all night?'

The barman nodded and headed for the door. He was on his way to fetch the town marshal.

* * *

Minutes later Ed was outside the law office, on his way to contact Dan and to make sure that he was up and about and in reasonable fettle to face a day's work. To Ed's surprise, Hector stepped out of the doorway and grabbed him by the arm.

'Good morning, Ed, did you by any chance see young Dan last night? He was down at the Silver Creek saloon celebratin', so I was told.'

' 'Mornin' Hector. Sure, I saw him fairly late on. The marshal an' me, we brought him along here to make sure that he got to bed all right without doin' anything silly to tarnish his reputation. Is there anything wrong?'

'I'd like to say there isn't,' the lawyer answered, with feeling, 'but the fact is Dan's left town. Accordin' to what I could learn from Reg Yarby, he ordered his horse to be saddled and ready and rode out without sayin' to anyone where he was going.'

There was a slight film of moisture above the lawyer's fair moustache. Ed noticed it; it was clear to him that Hector was shaken because Dan had left town so soon after being liberated. The detective grinned and patted his brother on the shoulder.

'Come now, Hector, take it easy. You have the look on your face of a man who has jest lost ten thousand dollars. Don't be so jumpy. If you want *my* opinion, either one of two things might have drawn Dan out of town. He might have gone to the Diamond L to see his mother, or he might have ridden to the county seat to give Walter McGurk a piece of his mind. You must have a little more confidence in your junior pardner, Heck. Now, go back in there and settle down to your briefs. I'll mosey along the town and see if there's anything known anywhere about Dan's present interests.'

As he turned away Ed had another idea. He thought that Dan might have left town to pay a surprise visit to Pearl Winder. He hoped that Dan had other things on his mind. The lawyer watched him walk away, and, after hesitating for a minute or two, he took the advice given and re-entered his office.

★ ★ ★

By the time Ed happened upon Dick Speed the body of the dead man was stretched out on top of the bar in the saloon. The barman had found something to do elsewhere and only Horace Black was keeping the peace officer company. Speed was smoking a thin cigarette, but Black was thirstily putting away his third whiskey.

Ed was bursting with curiosity, but he steeled himself to remain quiet until Dick was ready to explain. Black did not look as though he was capable of a few coherent sentences.

Speed, who looked very shaken, began: 'Who'd have thought it, Ed?'

Ed studied the figure from all angles. He was seeing a man he had never laid eyes on before. All that his detective's eyes told him was that the fellow had worn a moustache until quite recently. The flesh on his upper lip was definitely paler than the rest of his face.

Ed murmured: 'Bullet wounds. Three in number. Two close, in a vital part of the chest, and one higher, in the shoulder. Probably fired from fairly close.'

Speed rubbed his big jaw with the back of his hand. 'You an' I saw the bullets fired, amigo. Kind of makes us look foolish, don't it?'

In a flash Ed saw the implications behind his friend's words. He knew that the bullets had been fired by Dan Lawrence and that they had passed through the door and into the man's body. He moved around to the door, opened it, and examined the inside of it.

While he was doing so the marshal asked: 'Have you by any chance seen young Dan this morning, Ed?'

'No, Dick, and I don't figure either of us will today. I've been along to my brother's office, an' he was pretty shaken because Dan had left town on horseback in a big hurry. It kind of looks as if someone has told Dan what happened and that he has panicked. I told my brother there was nothing to worry about. Now I can see I was

94

wrong. The shock was too much for Dan. Two men dead by his guns. He must have thought that his luck had run out altogether this time.'

The uneasy saloon owner found his tongue. 'Tim Leeds, that's the fellow. He must have been the one to open the door and find the body. He must have gone straight along to Dan and told him what he had found.'

'If I'd been a young shaver of eighteen I would probably have done exactly the same,' Ed opined. He did not like the saloon owner.

Speed cleared his throat. 'Mr. Black, you look as if a bit of fresh air would do you good. Why don't you take a walk up the street and alert the undertaker and the doctor? You'd be doin' a public service. Besides, you don't want this stiff on your premises for much longer.'

As soon as Black had departed the other two got closer together.

'I've never seen this galoot before, Dick,' Ed began, 'but I'm guessin' now that you might have. How about enlightening me?'

Speed nodded, but he took his time in answering. 'Ten years back, in another town, this galoot went off with my wife. I haven't seen her from that day to this. I would have shot him if I'd caught up with him in the early days. Now I see things differently.

'His name, I'm not likely to forget, is Bummer Gorman. When I knew him before he had a moustache and no beard. Now he's supposed to be clean shaven. I think he had a nerve if he came to this town knowing I was the town marshal.'

Ed was quick to show sympathy. 'I guess he must have jest been passin' through, Dick. Nothin' more. He must have seen you come in through the batwings. That was enough. He made for the first door and went through it. Even though it was only a broom cupboard. You had him really scared, you know.'

Speed took the drink which Ed poured for him. 'That's about what happened, Ed. But it don't make me feel good to know he's dead. Fancy my wife takin' up with a no-good saddle-bum like that!'

Together they sauntered towards the door, where they awaited the arrival of the doctor and the undertaker.

7

At two in the afternoon two days later Ed Morissey was walking his distinctive buckskin horse along Main with an intent look upon his face. Slung over his shoulder was a short line with half-a-dozen small fish on it. He had spent the forenoon fishing in the creek rather than hang about in the office with nothing to do.

The lack of work bothered him. His rent for the office had to be paid by the end of the week and he had barely sufficient cash in hand to make the payment. Ever since Dan Lawrence had gone missing Ed had been at a loose end.

Now, as he rode, he was hoping against hope that he would find an impatient client sitting in his office or an urgent message to get in touch with somebody. There were not many people about in the street, but that was largely because of the searching early afternoon heat. No one was abroad, except those who had to be.

At last he came within a short distance of his office. He angled the buckskin towards the rail outside and studied the upper part of the glass window. Was there smoke behind the window, or was he just imagining it?

He dismounted, slackened the saddle with one hand, and walked quietly up the boards and into the office. There was an expensive-looking boot propped up on his desk. That much was obvious right away. Maybe he would not have to start cutting hair in place of Kopak after all.

The occupier of the main chair was his brother, Hector. In the metal ash tray was the butt of a cigar. The ash on it was two inches long. The lawyer was slumped in the chair, fast asleep. Ed studied him for nearly a minute and decided that his presence was a good sign. He then relaxed inwardly. A small retainer from brother Hector was better than no detective work at all.

Ed swung the fishes around and held them fairly close to the sleeper's nose. They were fresh water fishes, of course, but nevertheless the lawyer's sharp nose detected something. He rumbled a bit, twitched his nostrils and suddenly opened his eyes. He glared at the fish, which were at once withdrawn. Ed took them into the back room and returned before his visitor had the time to change his mind and leave.

'Good-day to you, Hector. A fine day for fishing. What can I do for you?'

'You can be in your office when I want you. That's the first thing. How do you expect people to bring you their troubles if you aren't here to listen to them? And whoever heard of a detective spending the morning fishing?'

Ed slid into the client's chair. He was in a relaxed frame of mind and he did not much care if his brother sounded off a little. Hector, who was hatless, ran his fingers through his thick cranial hair. He sighed.

'In three weeks' time I could be ruined,' he remarked uneasily.

Ed blinked. He removed his black stetson and hurled it at the hat stand, finding a hook but almost dislodging the other hat in the process.

He said: 'I could be cuttin' hair before the end of this week.'

'That won't be necessary,' Hector pointed out.

'How's that again?' Ed probed.

'I've paid your rent for another month. I'm engagin' you to work for me. Any objections?'

Ed chuckled and spread his arms in a magnanimous gesture. 'No objections at all, brother. Be my guest at any time. Always occupy the best chair. Why did you do it — pay the rent I mean?'

'I want you to do some real trailin'. You have to find Dan Lawrence. That's what it's all about.'

'Oh, that awkward young galoot. Is he still causing you headaches?'

Hector wagged a finger in Ed's

direction. 'You know darned well I signed my name to a paper guaranteeing his appearance in court when his case comes up. If he stays away that long I stand to lose ten thousand dollars. I can't afford it. Neither can I afford to lose face in the county by bein' made a fool of by my own junior. Don't you see how it is?'

Ed nodded. 'Yes, I think I do. His non-appearance wouldn't help you in your law business at all. I suppose you've checked that he isn't hiding on Diamond L property?'

'Both Mervin Hayes and his wife have sworn to me that Dan is nowhere around. More than that. He has not been in touch since he rode out in a hurry the morning Bummer Gorman's body was found. He's cleared out, given up, an' the frame of mind he's in he might turn to anything. I have to admit that the fellow is a little unstable. If he's fool enough to think his law office days are over anything might happen.'

Ed began to pull out his tobacco sack

from the side pocket of his corduroy jacket, but Hector forestalled him with the offer of a small cigar, which he accepted.

'Let's hope that Dan ain't one of those fellows who keeps on goin' in a straight line, otherwise I might not find him in time,' Ed observed.

'He's got to be found in time, Ed, or a very substantial reason given for his non-appearance.'

'What sort of an excuse would the judge take if he didn't appear?'

'He'd have to be dead, an' we'd have to show first-class evidence to prove it. Take it from me, circuit judges don't like their defendants to go missing. But I have great hopes in you, Ed. You can ride hard. You have lots of stamina, an' you can't deny your interest in the fate of Dan Lawrence. What sort of a rate are you goin' to charge me for your services?'

'Well, now, let's see. You've paid the rent already. How about three dollars a day and reasonable out-of-pocket expenses? Would that break you?'

Hector sighed. 'Not so long as you were back here inside the time limit. See this thing through for me, Ed, an' I'll see you get as much work as I can push your way after this. I mean that.'

The lawyer rose to his feet. He took a billfold from his inside pocket and left twenty-five dollars in notes on the desk. 'There's enough to start you off, but I'll expect you to be on your way without delay. Don't let me down, Ed, I'm in trouble.'

Ed was impressed by his brother's show of concern. He, too, rose to his feet and stood by the door to show his client out.

'I'll need what's left of today to make up my mind which direction to ride in. If he hasn't turned up again in the meantime I'll leave town first thing tomorrow.'

The lawyer gave his approval and left the building.

★   ★   ★

Ed rode north. His enquiries as to what direction Dan had taken after leaving town had not furnished him with much information. Placerville had been the first place he thought of after he woke up that morning. Most of the likely settlements were either north or east. If Dan had headed straight for a border he was likely to have ridden east, but Ed had a feeling he was nearer at hand, if he could only be located.

Placerville was a good day's ride, but Ed rode hard and made good time. It was early in the evening when his sweating mount carried him into the county seat, and by that time he was glad to get out of the saddle. He left the buckskin hitched to a rail with its saddle slackened. There was a water trough within reach, and he felt that the animal would not take much harm if it was given time to cool down slowly.

He walked a few yards and entered a cafe, where he ate a good meal of beef and vegetables, followed by fruit pie and coffee.

By the time he had finished everyone in town appeared to be relaxing, as was customary at that time of the evening. In order to goad himself into further effort Ed had to remind himself of the stricken look on his brother's face before he left. He knew that he would have to make a search of the busy part of the town before he looked for quarters for the night.

He was yawning in the fresh air when he came out again. A honkie-tonk piano assailed his ears and made him want to go in search of liquid nourishment rather than a wayward young lawyer with an outsize chip on his shoulders.

He shrugged, decided against the saloon with the piano playing, and instead set off in the other direction. The buckskin, once again carrying his weight, snorted a few times as though far from pleased with the resumption of the work. Ed leaned forward and briefly massaged the white blaze. He wanted to give the impression that he was in sympathy with his mount's feelings.

He studied all the hitch rails in the main street, and in the avenues opening off it. There were three fairly large liveries in the town, and he called briefly at each of them and asked after the grey stallion which Dan habitually rode.

In the first two he was curtly told that no such animal was in the stalls, and in the third a tired ostler invited him in to take a look himself. He found no signs of the horse, or anyone who had seen one answering to its description.

Having made what amounted to a circuit of the town, he then turned back into the main street and started to make his way slowly and carefully along its length. By this time he was assailed by doubts. He remembered how flimsy were his reasons for riding to the county seat, and his spirits flagged. In ordinary circumstances, and working for another client, he would not have worried so much. But he knew only too well that Hector was in trouble and that time was against him.

His mind's eye was seeing a simple map of the eastern half of the county as he approached the middle of the street. He was wondering which of a couple of towns to the east would be the next one on his itinerary and how many miles he would have to ride on the morrow. He had actually failed to scrutinise two small groups of hitched horses when the honkie-tonk piano cut in upon his thoughts again and drew him towards a saloon known as the Broken Wheel.

There were three groups of horses at one end of the frontage and a single restless animal pawing the ground at the other. To Ed's surprise and joy he saw that the single horse was almost certainly the one he sought.

He sighed with relief. For upwards of a minute he sat his saddle looking down at it and wondering what sort of a state he would find its master in. Only a relatively short time had elapsed since Dan's dash from Silver Creek. It was most unlikely that he had had a change of heart over his sudden departure. He would not want to see anyone in authority from Silver Creek, nor would he want to listen to advice.

In fact, he might duck away from a meeting with someone he knew altogether. Having found him, Ed did not want to lose him. He thought about ways and means for making sure that Dan did not make off in haste in the dying hours of daylight.

The horse was his weak point. Ed dismounted, hitched his own mount with the saddle still fairly tightly in place, and turned his attention to the fretting grey. It was the work of just a few moments to further slacken off the saddle. If Dan came out of the saloon in a hurry he would have to take time out to cinch up again.

Ed smiled to himself. He felt sure that he would find the elusive young man somewhere inside the Broken Wheel. He was hoping against hope that it might be possible to have a few glasses of nice cool beer before he had to come out in a hurry or make some other unsettling decision.

The big square saloon area was alive with men of all descriptions. The bar spanned almost the full width of it at the rear. About a third of the room was given over to round games tables with green baize tops. Smoke climbed steadily from pipes, cigars and cigarettes, forming a cloud under the ceiling which stained the wooden boards.

Another area was the one with the upright piano in its midst. There, the drinkers were intent upon the music. They formed a noisy section. Towards another corner there was a pot-bellied stove with a tall black chimney stack above it. Ed watched the glowing metal, but he drew his gaze away and walked up to the bar to avail himself of a drink before scrutinising the many faces on all sides of him.

A man on his own without a drink was always an object of curiosity in a western bar. Ed had no wish to draw attention to himself so he conformed.

His first beer was lukewarm, but he did not grumble. He paid for it, picked it up and sauntered over to the area where the card players were busy.

The bright lamps hanging over the tables made it easy to scrutinise the players' faces. Some were quite youthful, and others were almost hidden by facial hair, but young Dan Lawrence was not among them. Neither was he among the drinkers who had congregated around the piano player.

Ed gradually worked his way diagonally through the tables as though looking for a friend. He settled down at a vacant table quite close to the stove and called to a waiter who was passing by.

'Bring me three fingers of whiskey next time you are this way.'

The aproned attendant nodded and went off again, collecting empties and occasionally wiping down a table.

Ed was puzzled because he had not spotted Dan, but he was in no way downhearted. The odds were that the young fellow was somewhere inside this building. If he was not in the main part of it, then he was upstairs or in one of the rooms opening off it.

Time would draw him out. No man left his horse hitched outside all night. Ed felt that his luck was in and that all he had to do was keep on the alert for a while. His whiskey came. He paid for it, emptied the beer glass, and began to sip the stronger liquid.

Inevitably, sitting as he was near the warm stove, he began to feel relaxed. When the fiery liquid was half gone his eyelids began to grow heavy. He closed them for a time to rest his eyes.

8

The ground floor of the Broken Wheel possessed no less than three private gaming rooms. They were used by men who liked to take their gambling seriously. Often the games went on all night, and no one ever thought of cutting in upon a session and calling time. The only persons to enter were barmen or waiters, who were quick to answer a noisy summons, which usually amounted to a few sharp raps on a door panel with the butt of a gun.

Over the table where Dan Lawrence was busy there hung a big lamp with a wide shade above it. The round table was bigger than the lighter tables in the main part of the saloon. It was constructed of heavier wood and had a polished surface.

Dan was a good card player. Had he not been he would not have considered risking his slender resources on a game which he might well lose to men who were complete strangers. He had learned how to play cards in his law school, and some of the young men whom he had played with were much better card players than they would ever be lawyers.

He had started well, over an hour earlier, winning quite a few hands and considerably improving on the twenty dollars which he had had to start with. Now he was in rather a sorry position. His money, which had soared to nearly two hundred dollars, was gradually being whittled down, hand by hand. And he thought he knew how.

As his fingers were busy with the pasteboards his mind was active about his fellow card players.

He recollected when they had been hanging about the tables in the main saloon they had shown no sort of hurry to set themselves up in a private game. The man who called himself Bill had seemed aloof, and he had spent the best part of half an hour studying the hands of players. At times the only sign of life, apart from the restlessness of his hard grey eyes, was the thin cheroot which burned near a corner of his mouth. At first it had seemed that this man, Bill, had arrived in the saloon alone.

The other two, who answered to Hondo and Richy, acted as though they were well acquainted with one another.

Dan was now of the opinion that they all knew one another extremely well, but, in spite of his arriving at this conclusion, he could appreciate the differences in their respective personalities.

Bill, for instance, had developed a lively, talkative and shrewd personality. He had emerged as the leader of this bunch. He was a tall man in his late thirties. His broad face carried a narrow brown moustache and a slightly sardonic expression, which varied as the cards went down. His tall, tawny-coloured stetson contrasted with a red shirt and a black bandanna.

Hondo was a year or two older. He was the weighty one, a fleshy-faced individual with a deep, barrel chest and a straggle of dark beard. As he played he had a semi-permanent grin on his face which almost closed his eyes.

Richy was the one who acted and dressed most like a gambler. And yet the bulk of the money which was changing hands was not stacked up in front of him. He was the shortest of the trio, a mere five feet six inches, and slightly built as well. He had blue probing eyes in a lean, handsome face, the expression of which was always changing without giving anything away. He was clean shaven, and a delicate arc of scar tissue disfigured his left cheek. His dark curly hair was hidden by a round black hat. He had on a white shirt, a string tie, and a tailored black coat and trousers. He was also the youngest, being in his early thirties.

His fingers were long and restless. At times he did some rather fancy shuffling and dealing. Like the other two, he wore a neat gun belt which held two holstered guns. They did not look in keeping with the rest of his gear, and yet he gave the impression that he could use them if the occasion arose.

Dan was shaken out of a mild reverie when Bill put down winning cards, grinned at the assembled players, and at once began to rake in all the money from the centre of the table.

'My luck is in again, boys. Too bad I jest had the more powerful cards, Dan, otherwise things might have gone your way. You want another drink?'

The winner reached out for the whiskey bottle and tilted liquor into the glasses of Hondo and Richy, who took it with a good grace and smiling. They did not seem to be at all concerned that Bill was now winning steadily. Most of the time they appeared to be weighing up Dan, whose working capital had almost gone.

'Count me out,' Dan returned curtly.

The other three showed mild surprise. He was only referring to the liquor, but they were very interested in his apparent change in outlook.

Richy offered him a small cigar, but he rejected that and instead picked up a home-made cigarette which he had fashioned before the session began. He lit it with due care and turned a fierce gaze upon his fellows. His temper was mounting, but he was one of those who did not show it in the initial stages.

He cleared his throat when the cigarette was going. 'You boys have been holding out on me,' he said in a silky voice.

Bill pushed the cards to Richy and raised his brows in mock surprise. 'In what way, holdin' out on you, amigo?'

'I mean that it is now clear to me that you three know each other extremely well and that you probably came here together.'

Bill turned his hands palm upwards. He glanced at the other two rather apologetically and then beamed. 'My friend, is that important in a game of cards between friends?'

'It is if three of them combine to rook the other man, an' that's what you three have been doing since you made up your minds I wasn't to win. Richy, here, has been doin' some very slick dealin', and by the looks of things he's about to do the same again. Furthermore, it wouldn't surprise me at all if this deck of cards is marked, an' that's a pretty serious thing in the sort of games I play.'

Dan was thoroughly roused by this time, and he did not care unduly what his fellow players' reactions were going to be. Richy flicked a couple of cards in front of each of them and suddenly paused. Hondo appeared to be trying to coax knots out of his beard. Bill was the key to what was going to happen next. At first he smiled broadly. Next he laughed loudly, and his laugh was very slow to fade.

The odd man out could tell that something was brewing by the way the other two watched their leader. Dan knew he had roused them and that he had probably hit upon the truth about the marked deck, but that would do him no good now if they turned nasty.

He perceived that if he was to do himself any good he would have to take the initiative. He made up his mind in a few seconds, rising swiftly to his feet and drawing his one pearl-handled gun. The muzzle of the imposing-looking weapon wavered gently through a small arc which took in all three and finally settled on Bill, pointing at his chest.

All three men eased back a little from the table, but their hands stayed in view. They were acting like men who had been on the wrong end of a loaded weapon many times. Dan licked his dry lips and thought what he wanted to do and how best to do it.

Bill murmured: 'That's fighting talk in any language. What are you planning to do?'

'I aim to leave this room almost at once, and I am taking with me the full amount of money which I reckon I had won before you three started to cheat. If you don't agree to that you'll make a move, an' most likely it will prove unfortunate for you. I'd like to make it clear that I've nothing much to lose in makin' a bid for what I consider to be mine.'

Dan kicked his chair out of the way and moved forward, his eyes warily taking in every little move on the part of his enemies. Hondo and Richy looked far from pleased, but it began to look as if they would not try to draw unless Bill did something first, and he was only too aware of the steadiness of the hand that held the gun.

Dan lifted his hand a little, still keeping the gun trained very carefully. With his left hand he took off his hat and used it to sweep the money towards him. There were plenty of dollar bills as well as coins. Moving quickly, he scooped up many bills and tossed them into the hat, which he then lifted and rammed on his head.

'If I've taken too little I won't be back, gents, an' I'm sorry to cut short your game. Jest stay where you are until I've left the building and everything will be all right.'

He backed away to the door, listening with his ear to the crack when he got there. As far as he could tell he was not likely to run into anybody approaching the room. The trio, as he fumbled for the door handle, started to rise to their feet. He stayed long enough to dissuade them before throwing the door open and stepping through it.

He slammed it and stepped to one side. In spite of his lack of years he had a knack of knowing how to handle himself in these circumstances. He paused for a few seconds, but no bullets came through the panelling of the door. So he set off through the densely packed main room, which had filled up quite considerably since he retired to the smaller private room. His gun was holstered unnoticed.

As soon as the first two groups of standing men were between him and the door he began to breathe more easily. He rounded a couple of tables; eased his way behind a trio of men who were standing near and talking to the seated drinkers.

At that moment he turned to look back. He saw the door open and the three men emerge. It was clear from their tense expressions and the way they glanced around the room that they were intent upon chasing him. He was not to be allowed to get away with the money he had taken if they could help it. He made another five yards' progress towards the distant batwings before looking back again.

By that time the trio had split up. Bill was coming along the same route after him, while the other two had edged towards the sides of the room in an attempt to get around the drinkers and gamblers and head him off.

Dan jogged a man's arm, spilling his beer. He tarried about five seconds, trying to make the drinker believe that his action had been accidental. The affronted man was very doubtful about accepting Dan's explanation, but time was vital and the young fellow moved on again before further trouble had time to develop.

There was an open space just inside the batwings, and Dan was wondering whether his pursuers would risk taking a shot at him when he was clear of the tables. He was thinking that in just a few seconds he would know the answer to that query when a large party of men in trail garb began to surge through the swinging doors from the street.

Almost a dozen men were in the party. Already they had partaken of strong liquor in two other saloons. They were moving slowly and ponderously with their arms round one another's shoulders. The looks in their bloodshot eyes suggested that they would take on a whole army, or, failing that, all the drinkers in the Broken Wheel.

Dan dodged through the last of the tables while the newcomers were still surging in. He had the misfortune to lurch up against a great shaggy bear of a man, who was one of the foremost in the group still entering. At once he was pushed aside. Another man pushed him still further, and the jostling went on until he was three or four yards beyond the door and up against the outer wall.

He realised in a flash that the situation had gone sour on him. He would never penetrate the newcomers' party in time to elude his pursuers. Moreover, Richy, the dapper little gambler with the knife scar, was not more than ten yards away from him, coming around the wall. The gambler's blue eyes had a lethal look in them. The fingers of his hands were drumming light tattoos on the outer sides of his holsters.

Dan looked around. If he didn't do something entirely unexpected he was due to be caught. His eyes settled upon a wide window. It was not the sort that opened, but he was desperate enough to take a chance in going through a pane of glass. He reached it, jammed his hat more firmly upon his head, and determinedly ran towards it. A mere couple of feet away from the glass he leaned forward, threw up his arms protectively, and dived at the pane.

In a flash he was the focus of every pair of eyes in the building and of a good many more up and down the street.

He landed on the sidewalk with shards of glass flying in all directions. Some were sticking in his hat, others had penetrated the material of his shirt for a little way. He scrambled to his feet, hurriedly felt himself over, and made a dash for the grey, which, along with other waiting horses, had been rudely startled by the breaking of glass.

Dan knew his saddle was not very tight, but he leapt for it just the same. As he landed, so it swung away under him, dropping him in an untidy and shaken heap in the dirt. He grabbed his hat, which this far had stayed on his head, and scrambled to his knees. There was uproar in the doorway of the saloon as his pursuers fought to get through the small crowd of drunks.

Dan checked that his gun was still in the holster. He stood up beside his fretting mount and was about to do something about the saddle which had let him down when two swift revolver shots almost lifted his hat and ventilated his head.

The round black hat and head of Richy were showing through the gaping hole in the window glass along with the hand which held the gun. Dan ducked down low. He crawled under the stomach of his mount and gave his attention to the horse alongside of it. The buckskin, he could see, had been ridden well, but it was restless and ready to move off. And the saddle was already cinched up.

It was the work of a few seconds to loosen the reins, and he backed the animal into the street and leapt on to its back without any further mishap. By the time the trio had emerged he was about to round the corner of an intersection about one hundred yards away towards the east.

Ed Morissey, who had been asleep, emerged about a minute later. He pushed his way through the crowd which had gathered and listened to the gossip which was going on. He went close enough to see the grey stallion with its saddle draped in a strange position.

He realised with a shock that he should have been seeing his own horse, the buckskin, and that it was no longer there.

9

Ed stayed outside the saloon long enough to find out that Dan had angered three men in a private gambling game. Before he could have a private talk with this trio the town marshal started to saunter down the street with a shotgun swinging easily on his short thick arm. His appearance had the effect of sending them on their way. Their complaint, evidently, was not the kind which is taken to a peace officer.

Marshal Tiny Bradley kicked most of the glass off the sidewalk into the dirt of the street. He was a big-chested man in his middle thirties with arms like great hams and a wispy moustache. He pushed back a fringe of wavy black hair with his free hand and stood tugging at his one gold earring while he studied the hole in the window.

'Mercy me,' he remarked, in a voice

which sounded gentler than Ed expected, 'that hombre must have been in a hurry to come out that way. Another pane of glass gone, but I reckon the owner can afford it. He sells more liquor than anyone else in this town.'

He turned around and saw Ed holding the grey by the head.

'Something wrong with that stallion, mister?'

Ed shrugged. 'Only that he belongs to a fellow who took off in a hurry. He left town on my horse, so it seems I'm stuck with this one.'

Bradley nodded. 'Still, a strange horse is better than no horse at all. Any idea why the fellow went away in such a hurry?'

'A dispute at cards, judgin' by something I overheard jest now. Something that happened in one of the private rooms. Well, I don't figure on chasin' up the man on my horse right now. Maybe I ought to put this one in the livery and start in the morning. My horse can take to any good rider that treats him well, but this grey don't look at all happy with me. I'll maybe see you later, huh?'

The marshal nodded and grinned and moved into the Broken Wheel. Ed spent a minute or two thinking about his own changed circumstances. He had found Dan Lawrence, and he had lost him, and, in losing him, he had lost his own horse into the bargain. On balance, this had not been a particularly good day for him, even though he had located his quarry, who might have been miles away in another town altogether.

He considered the three liveries which he had visited earlier and selected as his own choice the one nearest the east end of town. He kept walking until he came up with it, and this time the tired ostler who had invited his inspection before was snoring in the hay scattered throughout the loft.

Hearing that snore reminded Ed of how tired he was himself. He found an empty stall for the grey, removed its harness and saddle, and gave it a rub down before finding a meal of oats in a bin at the rear. In all, he was in the livery about twenty minutes. Ten minutes after that he had found a hotel in a secondary street and a room which was barely furnished but which sufficed for a one-night stay.

He turned in after a brief wash and lay on his bed, smoking a last cigarette and pondering on how his next contact with Dan was likely to be. His eyelids were heavy before the smoke was burned down. He kept awake long enough to rub out the butt, and then he was sleeping fitfully.

A gentle knock on the door awakened him. He blinked his eyes open, peered through the window into the street to see how much daylight was still about, and decided that whoever was at the door had made a mistake.

He called: 'Go away, whoever you are! This room is occupied. Doggone it, I'm tryin' to sleep.'

A man with a voice he had heard earlier chuckled outside the door. 'Now that I've awakened you, Mr. Morissey, I'd be glad of the chance of a chat if you'd open the door.'

Ed yawned. It sounded more like a groan. 'All right, if you insist. It ain't locked. Jest turn the handle and walk in.'

He knew he ought to have guessed who it was, but he received a small surprise when the bulky town marshal catfooted indoors with his shotgun held like a toy. Bradley came across to the bed and sat down on the foot of it.

He extended a hand, which Ed shook quite firmly.

'You're Ed Morissey, the brother of Heck Morissey, the attorney in Silver Creek. After we'd parted company outside the Broken Wheel I got to thinkin' I ought to have known who you were, so, when I had a few minutes to myself, I made a check on the hotels an' I found a familiar name in this establishment's register. How's brother Heck keepin'?'

'He's in reasonable health, marshal,' Ed replied, propping himself on an elbow. 'Was there anything special you wanted to talk about?'

Bradley grinned. 'Your job is known to me, an' it interests me. I wondered if you were in the county seat on any sort of special assignment.'

Ed nodded slowly, but he was not keen to spread it around that he was working exclusively for his brother in seeking to get Dan Lawrence to go back to town. However, Bradley made it almost impossible for him to keep quiet about the assignment.

'Any thing to do with that Kopak affair, Ed? Were you by any chance tryin' to get in touch with anyone connected with the case? Like that young galoot whose gun fired the fatal shot?'

'You're well informed, marshal,' Ed conceded. 'I hadn't wanted to talk about the affair, but you've guessed most of the truth. Heck is worried about young Dan Lawrence. Dan left town in a hurry and my brother wants him back, with good reason. He has to answer a charge which will be made by Walter McGurk right here in this town. So you'll see that it is important for me to catch up with Dan before he gets into any more hot water. I have to take him back.'

'It must be an interestin' case, Ed,' Bradley remarked. He rose to his feet, and the bed straightened out as his weight was removed. 'You'll be wantin' to get on your way pretty early in the mornin', I guess. Here's hopin' you get on well with that grey stallion.'

In the doorway the big marshal paused and grinned broadly. 'If it's of any help to you, I've heard one or two reliable rumours that the runaway headed out of town towards the east. It's that way you'll have to go if you want to chase him. Goodnight, Ed.'

'Goodnight and thanks, marshal.'

Ed slipped back under his blanket and stared at the ceiling for a while. He had heard that Marshal Bradley was a good man at his job. Now he was beginning to know at first hand how the peace officer's reputation had been won.

* * *

Dan Lawrence rode the buckskin towards the east for upwards of two hours. For most of that time he was turning in the saddle in an effort to make sure that his enemies were not close behind him. Two hours' riding just about disposed of the remaining daylight, and that forced him to a decision. At the end of that time he stopped trying to figure out whether he had seen the buckskin somewhere before and started to think about the immediate future.

Ahead of him, and almost due east, was a town known as Butler's Ford. Unfortunately, it was at too great a distance for a man to reach it from the county seat in a short evening's ride. In fact, several hours of another day would be required to cover the distance to the town in question.

That meant that he would have to spend the night out in the open. Having regard for the attempted shooting after he had dived through the saloon window, he was not keen to bed down anywhere in an obvious place, otherwise he might find his pursuers up with him at a time when he was not ready to cope with them.

About ten minutes of semi-gloom showed that the trail was meandering a little towards the north in order to negotiate terrain which was far from easy for wheeled traffic. The blunt end of a gnarled ridge had loomed up to eastward. Acting upon impulse, Dan turned the buckskin off-trail and alongside of the ridge, still heading slowly eastward.

The animal protested, but he gave it a gentle touch of the rowel and it went ahead again. Presently the inky blackness behind the ridge began to affect his tired eyes. He found his eyelids growing heavy, and very soon he was dozing in the saddle.

For over a mile the buckskin continued to carry him. It was when it came to a sudden halt and pawed the ground that Dan recovered his wakefulness again and looked around him. There was no wonder that the tired horse had stopped. Barring its path now was a fairly wide, slow-moving stream.

It stretched across their line of ride from north to south and looked rather repelling in the darkness. A faint breeze blew along its surface. The young rider shuddered. He dismounted and decided that he would have to build a fire even though it might give away his position.

Fortunately there was plenty of loose kindling wood about. He gathered it up as quickly as he could and put a match to it. A few minutes' concentration ensured that the fire blazed. He then stood over it for a while, warming himself. He counted himself lucky when he found the makings of one or two trail meals in the saddle pockets of the borrowed horse. Soon he was eating a late meal of bacon, biscuits and coffee.

The food did him a lot of good at a time when his spirits were at a low ebb. For a time he walked around the fire with his coffee mug in his hand, weighing up the rather startling events of the day and wondering about the future.

He wondered now why he had dallied in the county seat. If the peace officers were after him for the accidental killing of the man in the saloon they might locate him at any time in such an obvious place. He thought he had been a fool to stay there for as long as he had. One reason why he had taken the risk was because there was no gossip of any sort in Placerville about the second killing. For a time he had thought himself safe.

At last he came to a halt beside the bed roll which he had taken from the buckskin horse. He unfastened it and spread it out, wondering if his sleep would be disturbed. A casual adjustment of his hat reminded him that there was something else inside it besides his head. The money!

He knelt down beside the fire and cautiously removed his headgear. He shook the notes out on to the grass and began to count them in the flickering light of the fire. They were in notes of one and five dollars.

The actual counting took longer than he anticipated. Presently he was past the two hundred mark and far from finished. His final total showed that he had appropriated almost three hundred dollars. Enough to make him feel that gambling could be a worthwhile profession. On sober consideration, however, he decided that he would have surrendered most of it to ensure freedom from arrest and to have undone the damage to his career which recent happenings had caused.

Eventually he slept with his wad of money down inside his shirt and a borrowed Winchester alongside of his head.

10

The rays of the sun were hot on his face and chest when he roused himself at a late hour the following morning. Birds were singing and the foliage in the trees alongside the water was moving gently, stirred by a gentle breeze.

A bird with brown plumage flew over him and dropped a twig which it had picked up for nesting purposes. He shook himself and decided that roughing it between towns could soon become monotonous if a man had too much of his own company.

The waters of the creek, under the sun's rays, looked blue and inviting. He had the means to refresh himself before moving on, and only the memory of the trio he had quarrelled with made him wonder if a delay for bathing was a worthwhile risk.

He kicked the embers of the fire into

life and prepared a breakfast which differed very little from his last meal. Soon he had eaten it. He smoked a cigarette while he looked around him for signs of pursuit. Having seen none, he made his way to the bank of the creek and started to pull off his shirt. His hat followed, and then his boots. Soon he was naked between two willows, with the sun playing upon his body.

He threw out his arms in front of him in a diver's stance, flexed the muscles of his legs, and dived neatly into the placid waters. Down he went to a depth of six feet, with bubbles trailing out behind him. Mosses grew up from the bed of the creek, and he found himself swimming through them like a fish.

Lack of oxygen drove him up to the surface. He threw out his head, turned on his back, and gulped in fresh air. As he peered upstream a small bird with brilliant blue and red plumage flew off a rock and crossed the waterway, alighting upon a similar rock near the other bank.

Dan made a series of surface dives, taking him down to the bed, where he browsed around until his lungs protested. He liked to swim and regretted that he had not had easier facilities for indulging in the health-giving exercises while he was at law school.

Thoughts of law school and the life which he had so recently abandoned to some extent spoiled his pleasure. He remained in the water for another ten minutes, crossing from side to side with a powerful overarm stroke which took him along at a fair speed.

At last he had had enough. He turned towards the bank from which he had entered and lazily swam along it, looking for an easy place to get out. Some fifteen yards above the spot where he had dived in was a small inlet with a gently shelving bank. He made for the spot, floated into it, and made contact with the earth.

He rose to his feet, his eyes screwed

tightly shut to squeeze out the water. When he opened them prior to going back for his clothes he was not alone. Grouped in an arc with one gun apiece levelled at him were the three faces he least wanted to see. Bill, Hondo and Richy had approached the bathing spot with great stealth.

He was impressed to see that they had found him, and not a little distressed about the latest turn of events. Acutely conscious of his nakedness, he put on a brave smile.

'Howdy, boys, you must have made good time in getting here. I figure I've put you to a lot of trouble. I guess it's no good suggestin' that you take a swim before we get down to the serious talk?'

The trio were not anxious to say anything, but their eyes, their general facial expressions, and their guns were full of menace. It occurred to Dan that if they had wanted they could have shot him where he was, right then, in the water, and departed with all his gear.

He had a new slant upon an old

saying at that moment. 'Where there's life there's hope.' He hoped he was not being too hopeful.

'Is it all right if I go back to my camp an' put on a few clothes, Bill?'

Hondo remarked: 'I think he looks real cute jest as he is.'

Richy's mouth quirked into a crooked smile, but the man spoken to grudgingly gave ground and pointed back towards the camp with his gun. Dan shook himself and set off rather gingerly across the grass on his bare feet. He was warming the front of his body at the fire when Bill tossed his clothing towards him and suggested that he should put it on without delay.

Dan dabbed himself dry and pulled on his shirt. As his face emerged he tried to draw his enemies out a little. 'If you've come for further discussions about the card money, I haven't spent any of it since I saw you last. I —'

'I know,' Bill retorted. 'I've already counted it. Now get your clothes on before we get tired of waiting, huh?'

By the time Dan had his trousers on and was struggling into his boots, all three men were round about him on a small circular patch of green grass beside the fire. Hondo, the bearded man, was the one who first took his attention. The fellow had found Dan's pearl-handled revolver and he was checking it over, detail by detail, as though he had decided to make it his own property. The redhead in Dan began to assert itself.

Some of his apprehension gave way to annoyance, and the annoyance to some extent was supplanted by anger.

He finished his dressing, apart from his jacket, and stood defiantly with his hands on his hips in the middle of the grass patch, alert to his enemies and anxious to know what they had in store for him.

'Well, boys, you've come a long way after me. I guess you ought to say what you have in mind.'

Bill crackled a small cigar between his finger and thumb. His sardonic expression never altered as he considered the recalcitrant young man in front of him.

'Surely you must have expected us to follow you when you snatched up about three hundred dollars of our money at the point of a gun?'

Hondo emptied the shells out of the cylinder of Dan's gun and dropped them on the grass. He was spinning the cylinder when Dan answered the question.

'I thought you'd make a move to do something about it, but I didn't think you'd find me this easily.'

Richy commented: 'It wasn't easy. We had to work at it real hard. So now we need some recompense.'

Dan felt bold enough to ask what sort of recompense they had in mind, but again Hondo distracted him. The bearded man had taken out his belt knife and he was shaping up to the pearl-handled gun as though he intended to carve his name upon the butt plate. Dan fumed at this. He took a quick look at Bill and Richy. They had both holstered their guns. The only revolver to hand now was his own, held by Hondo.

Dan stepped half a pace towards the hirsute man, who, he began to think, was deliberately goading him.

'I wouldn't like you to put any marks on the butt of that gun. It happens to mean rather a lot to me. Why don't you find something else to play with?'

Hondo slowly looked up, an aggrieved expression on his face. He tossed his knife in the air a few inches to change his grip and brought the blade point close to the butt plate. At the same time Dan moved still closer and struck down at the wrist of the hand which held the gun.

Hondo grimaced and let go of the gun, which fell to the floor at his feet. The bearded man was angered now. Besides, he had lost face in front of his partners. He fell into a crouch with his knife held handily in front of him. The redhead, he figured, had asked for trouble and nobody liked him sufficiently to interfere.

Dan glanced at the other two and saw a look of anticipation in their eyes. They wanted to see him humiliated. He faced in the direction of Hondo again, and narrowly avoided the first curving thrust of the knife.

Hondo cursed and came after him, flat-footed. The knife was flashing in the sun as thrust after thrust was made. In dancing clear of it Dan put himself within easy striking distance of the other two.

Quite unexpectedly, Bill thrust out a hand and pushed him in the back. Dan found himself propelled forward towards the knife man when he would have preferred to retreat. In order to avoid the next sudden knife thrust he had to grab for the man's wrist with both hands.

As Hondo came forward Dan stepped to one side and stuck out a leg. His adversary tripped over it and they both went down on the grass. Dan's grip on the wrist caused the older man to release the knife, but, in spite of that, Hondo was first on his feet. He shook Dan's hands off him and staggered up, breathing hard.

Dan was on the point of rising when a pointed boot, the property of Richy, struck him in the rear and sent him staggering into his opponent. Hondo hit him, but not with the full force of his arm. Dan moved back again, slightly winded and conscious that the other two were not prepared to let him fight singly.

The redhead threw two light punches and avoided a blundering rush. He was still breathing hard when Bill caught his shoulder, turned him round, and hit him in the chest. He backed into Hondo and managed to do him some little hurt with an elbow, but then Richy joined in, hitting him high on the side of the head.

Dan's senses swam a little; he had the sensation that he was spinning around in a circle, bouncing off the rugged fists of many more than three men. There was a roaring in his ears and his knees went weak, allowing him to sink to the ground when he wanted to fight on.

After that he keeled over, but that did not prevent someone from kicking him in the side.

The authoritative voice of the man known as Bill said: 'That's enough, Hondo! Richy, go and get some water. Hear me?'

★　★　★

Dan had no clear idea of how much time had elapsed before the round hat's contents had been tipped over his head. The water streamed down his face and entered his shirt around the collar. He blinked and opened his eyes, and it was as though he was still on his feet and circling within the other three.

The dizziness was slow to leave him. Dan sat up and put out a hand on either side of him. Bill gripped him around the neck and held a water canteen to his lips. He drank eagerly, and was pleased to find that the tepid liquor was laced with something stronger.

He murmured: 'Thanks, Bill, I needed that.'

A couple of minutes later he stood up and staggered off to the stream, where he threw himself down and stuck his face in the water. When he had refreshed himself he studied his reflection. He had collected a couple of bruises, one on his left cheek and the other on his forehead.

As soon as his legs felt steadier he retraced his steps to his tormentors, who were lying around only half interested.

'Well, boys, I guess you could say you had your revenge on me. What happens now? Do you have any special plans for the future? If so, how do they affect me?'

Bill motioned for him to sit down and, to his surprise, tossed him a small cigar. 'The future largely depends upon yourself, amigo. As a matter of fact, some of the things you've done since we met have impressed us. Like pullin' a gun on us when you knew we were cheatin' you an' the odds were three to one against. It takes nerve for a young galoot to draw against three men who have six guns between them and know how to use them.

'Another thing. The way you went out through that window at the saloon. It shows you don't necessarily panic in a tight situation. My buddies an' me, we get into tight situations from time to time. And now, seein' as how we ain't really been introduced properly, I'm Bill Collins. Sometimes known as Nevada Bill. Sometimes I get the full title of Nevada Bill Collins.

'Hondo, here, has forgotten his proper Christian name, but his other name is Mercer. An' Richy is Richy Lamotte. He's a French-Canadian by birth. Now it's your turn to talk. I've told you some things, an' I could be even more frank. But I'd like to hear how you come to be hittin' the trail on your own with a rather desperate look in your eye.'

Dan was sitting with his knees drawn up massaging the hurting spots on his ribs. Hondo and Richy both still appeared to be remote and a little bit hostile, but they were content for their leader to make all the running. Obviously whatever Nevada Bill said had to go with them.

The young redhead found that most of his hard feeling against the trio had softened during Bill's soothing talk. He wanted to know more about them and the way in which they lived. They were travelling men, like it seemed that he had to be, and they appeared not to have any trouble in making a living. The only way in which he could find out more about them was to tell about himself.

He began: 'A few short weeks ago I returned to the town of Silver Creek from law school in Tennessee. I was given a job by Hector Morissey, an attorney of some standing in the town. But I was restless and I found it a little hard to settle. Then, right out of the blue, two things happened to change the whole of my life.

'First of all, a man was shot with one of my guns, the other one which matched the one which Hondo was foolin' around with. The dead man was a known Peeping Tom, an' I couldn't altogether account for all my movements after the dance 'cause I drank too much punch an' I had to leave my girl friend to throw up.

'My boss backed me up in this matter an' I was released on his signing a document, although I still had to face a trial over the death. And then the other thing happened. I was celebratin' my birthday in a big saloon in the town. You know how it is. I was shooting my initials into a door. An' you'll never guess.'

Nobody attempted to guess. He had his audience's full attention for his narrative. After a pause he resumed:

'The door opened on to a broom cupboard, and the next morning a young man who cleans up in there found blood coming from under the door. There had been a man hiding in the cupboard. A complete stranger in the town. An' my bullets had shot him to death. When I heard about that I no longer expected anyone to believe I was innocent of the first killin', so I up before anyone came for me, saddled my horse and lit out of town. And, to cut a long story short, here I am. I'm lookin' for a new way of life.'

Dan was silent. He went back to the small cigar and derived some satisfaction from it. Nevada Bill was stretched out on his back with his tall dun hat pushed forward when he answered.

'Sounds like the story of how I got started on my present profession, Dan, boy. You'd never think it now, but I had well-to-do parents who paid for my training in an honoured profession. I, too, had a handy pair of guns, given to me by an admirer. One night I was pushed into usin' them. A man was killed and that was the turning point in my life.

'Folks like us, Dan, we're born two-time losers. Circumstances are against us right from the start. I'm glad you felt you could tell us about your own circumstances. The boys an' me, we travel a lot. I won't deny that we live mainly by the gun. But we don't stick around in one area long enough for peace officers to get to know us.

'I'll wager you've never heard the name of any one of us before we met. It jest shows that it pays to be careful in our line of business. Now, how would you feel about throwin' in your lot with us?'

While Dan was blinking with surprise Bill fished the big wad of notes out of his pocket. He peeled off the amount that Dan had first gambled with, and then doubled it. Having folded the notes over, he tossed them across to the redhead, who caught them and pocketed them without troubling to check on how much.

He said: 'Let me get this straight, Bill. Am I right in thinkin' that you an' Hondo an' Richy are outlaws, an' that you want to have me throw in with you, hit the owlhoot trail as folks say?'

Nevada Bill laughed, and for once he sounded as if he was enjoying himself. 'Sure, Dan, that's about the size of things. Four is a better number than three. We lost a man a short while back, in the adjoining territory. Now, what do you think about my proposition?'

'It's tempting,' Dan admitted, and in so doing he surprised himself.

He held off for a minute or more, thinking over all the time he had spent training to be an attorney, and here he was openly showing an interest in ruthless lawbreaking. He supposed that the attraction which he felt for Nevada's suggestions had to do with living dangerously. He also thought the outlaw leader had spoken a whole lot of good sense when he talked about certain men being born two-time losers.

'We wouldn't want you to go shootin'

at sheriffs and town marshals all the time. As a matter of fact, with careful plannin' it hardly ever comes to that sort of a shoot out. I think you'd be very useful to us as a front man, someone to go into a place, size up the possibilities of hittin' a worthwhile establishment, and find out what the snags are. Believe you me, our kind of work is a challenge. Only the best brains are good enough for it.'

Bill winked at him. The remark about brains had touched Dan's vanity. After another pause he had his reply ready. 'All right, if you don't push me too hard into offences against the person I'll give it a go.'

Hondo and Richy seemed a little dubious about his pronouncement, but Nevada was fully satisfied. They shook hands all round and began to make their simple preparations for moving on.

11

As a settlement Butler's Ford, the next town further east than Placerville, was a disappointment. It had only half the population of the county seat and none of the fine houses which graced the larger place on high ground. It lacked the shopping facilities, and its male population of workers was a mixed one.

There was a scattering of copper mines to the north and a few fairly large ranches in another direction.

Dan Lawrence approached the place on Nevada Bill's orders at two in the afternoon from the south-west. He looked down on it from the top of a hill slope about a furlong from the outskirts and thought that it did not have much to offer.

Hondo Mercer, who was riding with him on a mean low-barrelled pinto, grumbled when Dan stopped to concentrate on the view. The bearded man was troubled with perspiration under his beard and around his neck. He mopped himself rather ineffectively with a soiled bandanna and made it clear to Dan that he did not like riding in the heat of the day.

'Doggone it, Lawrence, are you goin' to sit out here in the heat all the afternoon? I'd jest as soon get into some shade if it's all the same to you.'

Dan grinned at him. 'Hondo, I have the feeling that you are not the best kind of travellin' companion for a horseback rider to have on trail. You'd put anybody's back up the way you go on about the heat! Why don't you ride on into town an' slake your thirst or something? I'm the one who's been charged to study the town, not you. So get off my back, will you, otherwise I won't be able to do a decent job!'

Dan turned away from Hondo and pulled out a spyglass to have an even closer look before riding the short distance into town. He was aware of the hirsute man glaring at him with looks that could almost kill, but he ignored the other's discomfiture entirely.

Some two or three minutes later Dan decided that he was ready to take a closer look at Butler's Ford. He telescoped the spyglass, slipped it into his saddle pocket, and nudged the buckskin forward.

Behind him Hondo cursed briefly and started his own mount in motion. A touch of contrariness made Dan suddenly ask for more speed. The buckskin shot away from the pinto and Hondo was left riding through dust some twenty-odd yards towards the rear.

During the hours when Dan had been with the trio as one of their number Bill had treated him well, Richy had remained neutral, and Hondo had still nursed a feeling of hostility from the time when the fight had developed over the pearl-handled gun. Dan thought that Bill had probably chosen Hondo to go along with him into town because he knew that there was no love lost between them.

Dan sent the buckskin across some waste ground and entered town at the western end. He glanced over his shoulder and saw that Hondo was contriving to keep him in sight. This made him even more determined to lose the bearded man, if only for a short while. So he rode on up the street for a few yards, rounded a bulky wagon with a patched canvas top, and hitched the buckskin to a low rail in front of two shops.

At once he slid out of the saddle, slackened the girth strap and rocked the saddle. Still screened by the wagon, he then walked back a few yards along the sidewalk and ducked into an alleyway which led into the next street. In Second Street he slowed down and began to get his bearings. On a bench seat, well back under the sidewalk awning, he slumped down and pulled out a tobacco sack. He rolled and smoked a cigarette and, all the time he was taking his ease, his eyes and ears were busy.

Not many people were about at that hour of the afternoon, but those who went by did not miss his scrutiny.

Meanwhile, on Main Street Hondo Mercer went into each of the two shops near the place where the buckskin was hitched without discovering where Dan had gone. Hondo was an impatient man at the best of times, and on this occasion his gigantic thirst had the effect of turning him away from his purpose after a very short time.

He abandoned his search for Dan before it was hardly begun and made his way to the nearest saloon, where he called for beer. So long as Nevada did not get the idea that Hondo had been slacking in his duties the bearded man did not care where Dan had gone. He felt certain that Dan would take an hour or more to do his survey so that he could impress Nevada with the thoroughness of his work. In that time Hondo figured he could drink four, or maybe five, beers without hurrying.

★ ★ ★

Some forty minutes later Milton Greer, a well-known figure in the town, started along the main thoroughfare from the telegraph office on his way to slake his thirst. Greer had been the town's telegraphist for over ten years. He was a tall, stooping man, with greying hair and gold-rimmed spectacles.

He was licking his dry lips and looking down at the boards when he walked alongside of the bulging wagon. The shadow it afforded him made him look up at it. There was a trade name painted on the side, but he did not really notice that because he was absently smiling to himself about something which pleased him. In ordinary circumstances he could not leave his job, but today he had with him in the office his son Wilbur, who was learning the job so that he could take up the same trade.

Wilbur was standing by, and that meant that Milton had an excuse for leaving his post to take on a most welcome glass of beer.

The telegraphist was still smiling when he emerged beyond the wagon and into the full force of the sun's rays again. He blinked, decided that his spectacles wanted a clean, and took them off his face to rub them with his handkerchief.

Quite by chance he found himself standing close to the buckskin with the white blaze. He frowned and pushed his rather homely face closer to the restless animal, while his fingers were busy with the white square of cloth. He held the spectacles in front of his eyes to see if all the dust was off the lenses. He was satisfied, but in doing this he got a close-up of the horse once again. His actions slowed as his memory began to function.

The previous day he had received a message sent out from the county seat by a man named Ed Morissey who had lost a horse. In the message the horse had been described as being a buckskin with a white blaze. And here was just such a horse, right under his nose!

He wondered if the Morissey fellow was offering any sort of a reward. The message had not said so specifically, but the address for anyone with information to offer was c/o Marshal Bradley at the county seat. That being so, there was definitely a possibility of a slight profit being made on this occasion.

Greer rubbed his long nose. He knew a few moments of indecision. Should he go straight back to the telegraph office and send off a message to the county seat or should he proceed to his favourite bar and first slake his thirst?

He gave the horse a long look, winked at it, and decided that the beer ought to come first. His beer intake was three glasses, and by the time he got back to the spot where he had seen the buckskin the animal had been moved. For a time he felt depressed, but then his spirits lifted. He had seen it and he knew that it had been in town, and that was all he needed to put in the telegraph message.

He squared his shoulders and walked off in the direction of his office with his mind busily sorting out the words to be used in the message.

* * *

Hondo was slumped over a table in a remote part of a saloon, the name of which he had not bothered to find out. Two things disturbed him. One of these was a strong ray of sun which had moved around so that it shone on him where he slept. The other was a small furtive-looking Mexican who kept digging him on the shoulder with a podgy whiskered hand.

The bearded outlaw blinked himself awake and muttered in a ill-tempered fashion. He shifted his chair and also hauled the table two feet to one side to be out of the sun again. The Mexican moved after him, patiently lifting his hat and waiting for the other's attention. 'Senor, I have a message for you. Please.'

169

This far the purpose for being in town had not been recalled to mind by the outlaw. He glowered at the man who was trying to talk to him and eventually put up a hand and grabbed him by the shirt front.

'An' I have a message for you, senor. You are a stranger to me. I don't want to know you, an' you are spoiling my rest. So vamoose, pronto, if you don't want me to toss you out of here.'

The Mexican stepped back a foot and meekly tried again. 'Senor, it is time for you to go. Already your friend has moved on. He said for me to tell you to make a move.'

This time Hondo's memory worked. He rubbed his eyes and blinked himself awake. 'You say my friend gave you this message for me? How did you know who I was?'

The messenger spread his hands imploringly. 'I was told to look for the owner of a horse of a certain description outside a saloon. A pinto horse is outside this saloon. You were pointed out as the owner. And now, senor, if you don't mind, I must leave you.'

Hondo looked as if he would have liked to give the poor messenger a cuff round the ear, but he was too late in getting into action. He watched the small figure in the steeple hat thread his way through the tables and move out into the open air. At last his thoughts went back to Dan Lawrence. Dan had tricked him. Would he, perhaps, inform Nevada that they had had no contact at all after reaching town?

He swigged the dregs of his beer, denied himself the pleasure of another glass, and came slowly to his feet. He wandered out, blinking hard in the bright sunlight and thinking what a nuisance it was to have to spend another night away from town. By nature Hondo was really a gregarious creature. He liked to make up for the lonely days and nights between towns by getting drunk in the company of townsfolk who know how to enjoy themselves.

He took his time in cinching up the pinto. Next he moved off down the street in search of the buckskin. It came as no surprise when he found that Dan had indeed moved on. All he could assume was that his charge would go away from town by the same route which they had taken to reach it.

He paused long enough for the pinto to refresh itself at a water trough and then he was on his way.

On the top of the hill to the south-west of town Hondo began to show signs of uneasiness. He was beginning to wonder if Dan would deliberately keep in front of him on the return journey so as to put him in bad odour with Nevada Bill.

Having sent the message about starting back, the young jasper should have waited. They had been told to ride in together, and they ought to return in the same fashion. Outlaws had to show respect for discipline, otherwise sooner or later they ended up behind bars due to their own indiscretions.

The outlaw halted his horse and began to look around uneasily. The surface of the ground beneath his feet was not of the kind which easily revealed horse sign. All his inclinations told him that Dan would have already gone beyond that point, and yet he could not be sure.

He was trying to make up his mind to do a couple of miles fast riding when an unexpected voice took him by surprise.

'Say, this hill sure is a fine vantage point.'

He was hearing Dan Lawrence's voice, and for a minute or more it was not at all clear where the young man was located. Hondo was still looking around furtively and trying to avoid asking the obvious question when Dan whistled. The buckskin had been with him long enough to know what he wanted. It strolled up a slope beyond the tree stand and came to a halt under the tallest tree in the area. While it was there Dan dropped out of the tree, slipping from a tree branch and alighting in the saddle.

'Lawrence, I'm gettin' a little tired of havin' dealings with you. Men in our line of business don't play hard to get like you do. I don't think you're cut out for one of us. You'll louse up the first job we go on, an' then we'll be finished as a team.'

Dan chuckled. 'One of your biggest troubles, Hondo, is that you were born a pessimist. That means you always tend to look on the black side of things. I've been busy ever since we parted. I doubt if you could say the same. Anyway, it's time we were movin' on an' that's for sure. Are you ready?'

Hondo seethed for a whole mile. At the end of that time he felt he ought to know more about what Dan had been doing, otherwise he would cut a poor figure when they got back to camp.

He said: 'I figure you were busy mostly in the west end of town. What did you find out?'

'Quite a lot of things,' Dan replied easily. 'Not much to put us in business, though.'

'How do you mean?' Hondo asked cautiously.

'Well, the only commercial concern which took my eye was the Eastern Territory Commercial Bank, and I didn't think a lot of that. As a matter of fact, I found out that it is little more than a one-man establishment. The president does all the counter work, and the only other person working there is a spotty-faced youngster in his middle teens. I don't figure the president has any more to spend than you or me. So it wouldn't pay a professional outfit to hit his bank. It wouldn't be worth the risk.'

Hondo nodded. He was impressed with Dan's summing up of the situation. However, in an effort to get more information out of him, he asked another question. It amounted to a shot in the dark.

'But you weren't watchin' the bank

all the time, were you? What was your other interest?'

Dan was surprised in his turn. He began to wonder if Hondo had witnessed some of his activities after all instead of propping up a bar the whole of the time.

'You're right, pardner. The other place I went along to see was the store which distributes the weekly newspapers. But I was a day early. The paper that serves this territory won't be on sale till tomorrow afternoon.'

Hondo shot him a shrewd glance. 'If you've turned your back on your past why do you want a newspaper?'

'I have to be sure that my past doesn't catch up with me, otherwise it might bring trouble, unwanted trouble, to my new pardners.'

This explanation satisfied Hondo. He thought Dan had a point there.

12

Ed Morissey, whose morale had been on the low side since he missed Dan Lawrence in the county seat, walked Lawrence's big grey stallion into Butler's Ford in the early afternoon of the following day.

Ed had left Placerville long before Milton Greer's telegraph message reached the office of Marshal Bradley, but the peace officer had not thought this a bad thing because he knew that Ed was already on his way to Butler's Ford.

Around midday Ed had taken time out from his riding to rest himself and the horse and to take a light meal. While he was off the trail the stagecoach from Placerville had gone through at a fair speed, and, although he made a start shortly after it had gone out of sight, he had still not overtaken the vehicle before the next town loomed up.

The grey was steaming through its protracted efforts, and Ed had perspired a lot himself by the time he located the first livery at the western end of Butler's Ford. He stopped the grey outside the stable and remained in the saddle long enough to knock the dust out of his blue shirt and off the flat crown of his hat.

Having dismounted, he hitched the grey to the nearest rail and entered through a small door, searching for the man in charge. Slim Grant, the man he sought, had just taken off his leather apron and put on his jacket and hat. Slim was a lean, bow-legged individual in his forties with widely spaced teeth.

Ed said: 'Good-day to you, mister. I've got a rush job if you could do it for me. There's a grey stallion outside. He's a bit blown. I'd like for him to have a thorough groomin' and a light feed. My circumstances make life a little difficult. I might have to move on again in a very short space of time.'

Slim started to grin and to shake his

head, flashing his tobacco-stained teeth. 'Mister, you sure have picked a bad time for a rush job. You see, the stage arrived in town jest a short while ago. Me, I have the habit of walkin' along to the other end of Second Street to collect the weekly paper from a store. It always comes in on the coach at this time. Now, if you care to wait for half an hour I'll be glad to oblige you. You'll allow the weekly delivery of the newspaper is something of an event in a small town.'

Ed listened well. His initial annoyance gave way to a lively interest in the arrival of the newspaper. It was just conceivable that this week's *Rockland County Gazette* might have a bearing on the case he was working on. And, what was more, the elusive young Dan Lawrence might also want a copy. The distribution point might be a very good place to keep watch for the missing man.

Ed beamed. 'I can see you like reading the news as much as I do. Why don't you let me go along to the store and collect a paper for you? I'll buy it for you as well if you'll break your routine jest this once and groom my horse!'

Grant was obviously tempted. He pulled off his hat, scratched his thinning cranial hair, and yawned. Ed rolled a smoke and offered it to him. He took it, and the bargain was agreed upon. A minute later the newcomer was on his way up the sidewalk and the tired grey was being led into the stable.

Ed found the store in question without any difficulty. It was a general store run by the Gallon brothers. Because of the distinctive smell of newsprint the newspapers were kept well apart from foodstuffs on a counter at the far end of the building.

Zack Gallon, the older brother, a tall fifty-year-old with a short bristling moustache, was himself handing out the newspapers and taking the money. After every other sale he paused long enough to wipe his rather damp hands on the front of his white apron.

Ed received his two copies and paid for them. He coughed to keep the shopkeeper's attention and gave him a smile. 'Pardon me, mister, but I'm tryin' to catch up with a ridin' acquaintance. A youngish redheaded man on a buckskin horse. You wouldn't have seen him in here since the papers arrived, would you?'

Zack, who had a poor memory for faces, shook his head in a rather expansive fashion. 'I can't say that I've seen your friend, but, then, there was quite a rush for the first score or so of copies so I might have served him and not noticed. Sorry, friend, I can't help you.'

Ed said that he understood. He added: 'If anyone answerin' this young hombre's description should happen along this afternoon would you be good enough to tell him to stick around, because a friend is lookin' for him?'

Gallon started to shrug, but Ed dropped a silver dollar on the counter and the shopkeeper had second thoughts. Gallon picked up the coin and nodded several times. He was frowning as Ed left the shop. His rather slow brain was trying to memorise the description given to him.

Out in the street Ed exercised his senses, but nothing he saw or heard seemed to suggest that Dan Lawrence was in the vicinity. He shrugged off his mild disappointment and turned his attention to the newspaper. Having pocketed the liveryman's copy, he perused his own.

Down the front page there were two or three highly sensational articles which did not hold his attention. The stuff he was hoping to find turned up on an inner page. A brief glance showed that his troubled brother had not been altogether idle in the last day or two.

The first notice read as follows: —

Daniel Lawrence, of Silver Creek, Rockland County, New Mexico territory, is requested to return to or immediately get in touch with the office of Hector Morissey, attorney-at-law, in Silver Creek.

Mr. Lawrence is assured that the unfortunate event which occurred on his birthday is not likely to affect his career in any way whatsoever.

A second, smaller, item lower down the column was also of interest:

Will anyone knowing the where-abouts of Daniel Lawrence, Esq., of Silver Creek, please get in touch with Hector Morissey, attorney-at-law, Silver Creek?

Having read both items, Ed lowered the paper and hastened his step. He was reflecting that Hector had risked Walter McGurk finding out that Dan Lawrence was missing. He wondered if Heck had been wise in making his plight known to a wide public through the newspaper.

Slim Grant took a pride in his work.

Having agreed to break with routine and groom the grey stallion, he did a very thorough job. He needed another five minutes to complete it when Ed arrived back, and the latter was directed to take his ease in the office until the work was done.

Presently the stable hand was satisfied and he began to replace the trappings. Ed came out and watched him. As soon as he had finished he drew attention to the second copy of the weekly paper stretched out on the desk, paid the bill, and shook hands.

Perhaps another fifteen minutes had elapsed when Ed arrived back at the Gallon store and dismounted. Zack Gallon saw him before he was properly through the door.

'Did you see him?' he bellowed.

Ed shook his head, but his interest remained. 'You mean he's been in here since I left?'

'Sure, not more than five or ten minutes ago. I told him a man was lookin' for him, an' I'd have sworn he was waitin' right outside the store. He can't be far away. Take a look around, why don't you?'

Shortly after that the store was temporarily empty. Zack came out on to the sidewalk and looked around him in a puzzled fashion. He followed Ed to the nearest intersection and looked up and down in both directions.

He was murmuring: 'Red hair, an' a buckskin horse and all,' and shaking his head when the sudden emergence of a horse and rider from a street further north filled him with excitement. He pointed up the intersection to where the rider was turning his horse so as to go still further north, away from them.

'Hey, you with the red hair! Hold on a minute, your buddy is here!'

The figure on the horse, who was in fact Dan Lawrence, turned and briefly looked back, but, having done so, he gave his horse a touch of the rowel and went away at a greater speed instead of waiting. Ed, who was on foot, gripped Zack's hand and thanked him.

'Save your breath, amigo, I guess he's a little shy. But I'll be able to catch him up. Maybe I'll see you again some time.'

Ed ran back to the grey, hastily threw himself into the saddle and came back to the intersection, where he took up the pursuit with Gallon watching him. Dan was putting up a good pace. Obviously he was not at all keen to be overtaken. But Ed was just as keen not to be shaken off.

The pursuit took them out of town on a climbing trail for half a mile or more. A little way beyond the high point a small secondary track led off to the left over the rim of a pleasantly shaded hollow. Ed waited a minute or two, decided that Dan had turned off, and sent the grey into the hollow.

He hauled the animal to a halt in timber thick with foliage. Ahead of him, across about fifty yards of open ground, stood a solid-looking rough log cabin with an ill-fitting door. The buckskin was out of sight, but Ed would have gambled that it was not far away. For his money, Dan was somewhere around that shack.

After looping the reins over a branch, Ed made his way as far as he could in timber cover, and then he darted out and ran across the open, making the minimum of noise. He paused, slightly out of breath, peering through the gap caused by a broken hinge. His instinct still told him that he was not alone, but he could see no signs at all of anyone having recently entered. Ed found himself fingering his holster, but he reminded himself that he was dealing with young Dan Lawrence and not a wayward gunman.

He called: 'Anybody in there?'

Receiving no reply, he stepped through the open door and peered around him. There was a table and a few chairs and stools, also a couple of bunks against a wall and lots of shelves. He was peering down at the beaten earth floor when the revolver clicked and drew his startled gaze up to the loft, which spanned half the length of the dwelling.

Just showing over the open end of the loft was the pointing six-gun and behind the weapon Dan's head, from the eyes upwards. Dan blinked, but did not react in any other way for several seconds. Faced with this threat, Ed slowly hoisted his hands and waited.

'Ed Morissey! You of all people! How come you are all these miles from home an' chasin' me around?'

Ed grinned. 'If I wanted an excuse, you are the galoot who misappropriated my horse in the county seat. Ever since then I've had to make do with that broken-winded stallion you left behind, an' that's no joke!'

Dan began to protest, but he thought better of it and lowered the gun. He did not seem at all pleased to know that Ed had gone to a lot of trouble to find him and make contact. Ed backed off and sat down at the table, pushing the legs of his chair into the soft floor. There Dan presently joined him, accepting a smoke with a bad grace.

'You shouldn't have come, Ed,' Dan advised him. 'I may have left in a hurry, but having done so I want to stay away. I've read what your brother had to say in the paper, but it's clear to me that he wants me back so that he'll save his ten thousand dollars. That's all he's interested in.

'That second episode in the saloon is bound to influence any jury at my trial. I jest won't stand a chance. So I'm not goin' back. Please don't try to argue about it. I've taken up other interests.'

Ed spread his hands and looked down at them. 'Dan, I'm in a unique position. I could have been my brother's junior pardner, only I kicked in my training before I qualified. Be advised by me before it's too late. Everyone knows that business on your birthday was a pure accident. The fellow was a free loader. When he saw the marshal, something that had happened earlier in another town made him duck out rather than face him. He entered the cupboard by mistake. No one could possibly have guessed that a man was hiding in there.

'This far all the harm you've done in the world is steal my horse, an' I'm not aimin' to bring charges. All I want is to have it back. Now, why don't you collect it and ride back with me? What do you say?'

'I say no, and I asked you not to argue with me, Ed. Why don't you leave now an' let me lead my own life? You'll admit I've had bad luck. So leave me in peace. I don't want to know about Heck Morissey, or about Silver Creek for that matter.'

Dan sprang to his feet and started pacing the floor. Ed got up a little more slowly and strolled in the general direction of the door.

'Dan, drifting is not a good thing for a young man with your outlook. I can't let you go on like this. Before you know where you are you'll be permanently on the wrong side of the law.'

Ed took up a stance just inside the

door with his hands on his hips. He was making it clear that he was prepared to stop Dan leaving if he would not co-operate.

Dan saw what he had done, but he went on pacing for a time or two more. He sighed, slowed his walk, and approached Ed rather diffidently. It appeared that he had decided to co-operate. The younger man thrust out his hand as though to shake hands. Ed relaxed in turn and moved to take the hand. At the last moment Dan drew his hand back, bunched it into a fist, and drove it into Ed's midriff.

The detective was robbed of his breath and he doubled at the waist in considerable pain. Dan tried to get behind him and out of the door, but Ed fought off a feeling of nausea and remained in the way, throwing a couple of punches which lacked power.

Dan bored in first from one side and then from another. Very gradually Ed was recovering from the first underhand punch. He was contemplating leaving his post and doing a little chasing when a heavy object crashed down on the back of his head and at once robbed him of his senses.

★ ★ ★

Doing things quietly always put a strain on Hondo Mercer. He was breathing hard as he stepped over Ed's inert figure and looked down at him.

'Who's this, an' how did you come to lead him out here?'

Dan started to make light of the matter. He was smiling when he answered. 'He's a nobody. He owns the horse I borrowed back in Placerville an' he came after me lookin' for it. A man in the store said someone was lookin' for me, so I led him out this way to find out who it was. He won't bother us again.'

Mercer had pulled his gun and looked as if he would have been better pleased to use it on the fallen man. 'If we have to come back to this town on business this hombre might be a nuisance.'

'We won't be coming back here, Hondo. There's nowhere worth robbin'. And besides this man won't hang around. He'll be ridin' back westward as soon as he locates his own cavuse. It's round the back.'

Grudgingly, Hondo nodded approval. Nevertheless he gagged Ed with an old piece of cloth, found on a bunk, and used some leather thongs to truss his ankles and wrists. Dan did not want Ed to suffer particularly, but he had to put on an air of indifference, otherwise Hondo would not have approved.

When they moved on again Dan was riding on his own horse. Hondo thought that he was particularly quiet.

13

Around seven o'clock that evening, in a snug night camp not far from water, Richy Lamotte was playing a trapper's lament on his twanging mouth harp. Five yards away from him Nevada Bill Collins was flapping a piece of cloth so as to create more draught to boost the fire. The camp was nicely situated some five miles south-east of Butler's Ford.

The French-Canadian, who had been playing for over half an hour, stopped quite abruptly, took the small instrument away from his face and fingered his cheek scar. Nevada glanced over his shoulder to know what was happening.

'Are you sure you aren't puttin' too much confidence in that young red-head, Bill? You surprised me when you sent him back into Butler's Ford for another look around. After all, you can't be altogether sure he isn't cooking up trouble of some sort?'

The tall man straightened up, wiping his hands on his black bandanna. 'It's all right to be cautious, but only up to a point, amigo. I'm not altogether certain of young Lawrence, but we shall know a whole lot more about whether to trust him when he reports back tonight. Don't worry about him.'

Lamotte appeared to accept Nevada's assurances, but when he was about to play his instrument again Bill stopped him. Someone was approaching. They both moved swiftly and quietly away from the fire and were nowhere to be seen when Hondo and Dan covered the last fifty yards on horseback.

Dan dismounted first, but Hondo stayed in the saddle, looking around for the other two. The latter said in a conversational tone: 'It's all right for you to come out, boys. There's jest the two of us, an' we don't have anybody on our back trail.'

A minute later Nevada and Richy

came out into the open, one from either side. Each of them was toting a rifle. It was Nevada who walked up to the other two and gripped them by the shoulder and slapped them on the back.

Lamotte accepted the role of cook. He picked up Dan's newspaper and read parts of it while he was busy. Meanwhile the other three settled down behind a fallen tree and began to talk.

'Everything go all right?' Nevada asked.

Dan was about to answer but Hondo beat him to it. It was then that the young redhead saw that Nevada's eyes were really on Hondo.

'I guess it is. Lawrence went off to a store to buy a paper an' after that he moved out of town to an isolated shack with a stranger following him. I tailed the pair of them and pistol-whipped the stranger when they were having a fight in the shack. I would have shot the stranger but Lawrence seemed to think he wouldn't do us any harm.'

Nevada shifted his hard grey eyes to

Dan, who was quick to give his explanation. 'The fellow in question was the owner of that buckskin I borrowed back in Placerville when we first met. Quite by chance he happened upon me again in Butler's Ford. We left him trussed, and he would find his horse when he got loose. That was his sole reason for being that far from the county seat. Shall I talk about the other matter now?'

Nevada glanced in Hondo's direction. The latter shrugged, and so Dan was permitted to continue.

'As a town Butler's Ford doesn't have very much to offer for the likes of us.'

Dan was giving his findings boldly and his manner impressed Hondo. Richy Lamotte also looked away from his cooking. The tone of voice had drawn his attention.

'There are three fairly big stores, but none of the storekeepers is making a fortune. I told you about the Eastern Territory Commercial Bank yesterday. At the other end of town the Cattlemen's Trust Bank has a bigger, better, building, but the volume of business which it does is no greater.

'I talked to one or two people who knew the place well. The manager looks as if he has only one suit. He likes horses and recently he had to close down his own small stable and sell his riding stock. This is surely not a sign of prosperity.

'Butler's Ford is an in-between town. It won't ever rival the county seat to westward, and the next town further east has the advantage of being near the border with Texas. The place is called Hardrock Springs. You told me once that you do not strike jest for the sake of strikin'. My advice would be to try the next town.'

Dan stopped talking and he had apparently finished. Nevada toyed with a small cigar. Hondo shifted his sitting position uneasily, and Richy tossed aside the newspaper and gave more of his attention to the frying pan. At last

Nevada showed his frame of mind.

'I'm impressed with all you've said, Dan,' be began, his cynical grin back on his face. 'As a matter of fact, I already knew that Butler's Ford was not for us. I had advance information about it from an acquaintance some time ago. What's more, we shall be goin' on to Hardrock Springs. That's where I've always intended to make our next strike.

'As a matter of fact, I have a contact in one of the banks there. Knowing him will probably make our strike a little more safe for all concerned.'

Lamotte was clattering plates, putting out beans and bacon on them for four men suddenly hungry. This caused a slight pause in the discussion. Some ten minutes later, when all the plates were empty, Nevada resumed.

'Hardrock does trade across the border, as Dan, here, has already surmised. We shall probably hit the bank early in the afternoon. All being well we make a quick getaway towards the east. That way lies the border. Most raiders runnin' for the border don't stop until they've crossed it.

'My plan is to make the Texas Creek, a water course which lies across our path, before nightfall. We cross it, do a mile or two along its further bank and then double back, further south. If we cover our tracks the pursuit will ride straight on towards the border.'

At this stage an excited discussion developed. Dan could not deny that what he had heard had set his pulse throbbing. He listened to the others, taking in every detail. He wanted to ask his own questions and yet he held back, knowing that most of them would sound naive.

After a time the conversation began to flag. One after the other the trio glanced in his direction.

Lamotte asked: 'What about Lawrence? Is he coming into the bank?'

Nevada studied Dan and then glanced at Hondo. He figured that the bearded man was equally curious to know about Dan's role on his first strike as a renegade.

'Dan stays outside. He will be the horse minder.'

Dan was acutely aware of the eyes of the others upon him. 'May I ask if you don't want me in the bank?'

'Somebody has to look after our line of retreat,' Nevada observed.

'The horse minder is very important, especially if anything goes wrong,' Lamotte remarked. 'Sometimes he is the first to know of approaching danger. He has to keep his nerve if we are to get out without trouble.'

Dan nodded, several times. He was showing signs of acute restlessness. About five minutes later he asked permission to withdraw from the discussion and went down to the water to bathe.

As he swam he brooded over this vital step. He knew that if he had to use his gun it would be to deter anyone from seriously interfering rather than to shoot anyone down. It occurred to him that if Ed Morissey turned up again the detective could cause a whole heap of trouble for the two of them.

The bathe revealed that the last of his small cuts, caused by glass, had healed, but he took no comfort in the knowledge.

★　★　★

The business of cutting himself free from the cords which Hondo had used on his limbs took Ed almost one and a half hours. For thirty minutes he crawled around the shack like a crab, trying to locate some sort of a cutting instrument. He found none. Hondo had taken his knife and revolver when he trussed him up, and there was no sign of either anywhere around.

It was only when Ed abandoned the shack and began to crawl on the grass outside that he began to make progress. His wrists and ankles were aching and he felt half choked when he happened upon a rusting tin can which had been tossed out of a rear window.

The lid had been opened with a knife and the edge of the tin was jagged, but it did not easily cut through the leather thongs. Ed felt considerably older and thoroughly out of sorts with himself by the time the bonds parted and his wrists were free.

His skin was chafed and he took a well-earned rest before tackling his ankles in the same way. Although he did not have to struggle any more to get into a good cutting position, his efforts dragged on. Half way through he chewed a bit of grass to ease the dryness of his throat.

After that he strained to pull his ankles apart while he sawed with the tin. At last the thong parted and he was left to stand up in the ordinary fashion. He walked backwards and forwards, his thoughts quite a long way from Dan Lawrence and the man who had struck him down from behind. For a time he was only concerned with his own needs.

The water in the shack was stale and

brackish. His first task was to find out if a horse had been left anywhere near. The expert trussing made him doubt if he was due for any lucky breaks, but his spirits rose when he discovered the buckskin cropping grass in a saucer-like hollow less than a furlong away.

He drank from the water canteen and rejoiced when he found his gun and knife tossed down in the grass. If only that knife had been left a little closer he would have been saved a whole lot of trouble.

Gradually he began to recover his sense of proportion. He rolled a smoke and sat on the back of the buckskin sucking at it until it was almost gone.

Now he was able to consider Dan Lawrence again. Dan had deliberately drawn him out of town as far as the isolated shack. He had found out what Ed had come after him for, and, when he had heard everything, he had shown quite clearly that he had no intention of coming back to Silver Creek, except under duress.

Ed did not think that the man who had struck him down was the owner of the shack. The building had not been lived in for some considerable time. Very likely the unseen man had been Dan's partner, or one of his partners. Ed remembered the way in which Lawrence had left Placerville. He now thought it quite likely that Dan had taken up with men on the wrong side of the law. A wild bunch.

He started the buckskin off in the direction of town. As he rode he tried to put himself in the position of Dan. Either Dan, or the other fellow, had so trussed him that his escape could only be achieved with considerable delay. They had not wanted him to be in a position to trail them again straight away.

They wanted him off their backs, but for what reason? Were they hoping to pull some job in Butler's Ford, or did they merely want a few hours in hand to get clear of the town? If they were moving on, where were they heading for?

As Ed made his enquiries in the town he gradually became calmer but at the same time more frustrated.

It soon became obvious that no sort of robbery had been perpetrated in Butler's Ford that day, and it began to appear as though nothing was planned for the remaining hours of daylight. Ed searched systematically and asked questions. He had been in town for exactly one hour when Zack Gallon, the storekeeper, caught sight of him and called him over.

'Did you find that redheaded friend of yours? Don't say he gave you the slip!'

Ed grinned broadly and secretly felt the bump on the back of his head where the revolver had hit him. 'He gave me the slip, Mr. Gallon. I guess you must think we're playin' some fool game, but it ain't that at all. I have to convince him about takin' a certain course of action an' he's young an' headstrong an' he don't want to do it. Do you happen to have seen him again since I lit out of town after him?'

'I surely did. He rode out of town quite some time ago with a man I hadn't seen before. A fellow with a beard. They took the trail towards the east, if that's any help to you. Right now I'm busy. I have to go indoors, but I wish you luck with your search.'

Ed thanked him and turned away, his mind full of turmoil, his feelings mixed. It seemed that Dan was not likely to take an unredeemable step in Butler's Ford. Everything depended upon happenings further east. He was beginning to feel now that Dan needed help as much as his brother, Heck, did.

There was more riding to be done on the morrow.

14

Hardrock Springs was said by those who passed through to be a town of character. One of the reasons why it prospered was because it welcomed visitors from across the border. Its hotels gave good service and this helped towards prosperity.

It differed from a lot of other western towns in that it had a square. On one side of the square was a building which had once been started as a church. Its side walls were adobe-built, and it had a square tower above it which had intended to house a bell.

Unfortunately a dreaded decease had killed off the devout men who had started the construction, and the building — at a much later time — had become a saloon. Ed Morissey located this saloon within half an hour of arriving in the town on the second morning after his last meeting with Dan Lawrence.

In the coolness of its interior Ed had hastily downed a glass of beer. A man in a white overall was about ready to go up a flight of wooden steps towards one wall with a bucket and a mop. Recent conversation near the bar suggested that the owner of the saloon was thinking of opening up the old bell tower as a tourist attraction.

He hoped to popularise the spot as a place to view the town; if it caught on it might conceivably become a source of useful revenue.

Ed moved up to the bar and nodded to the owner, a rotund fellow with black hair parted and brushed forward. 'Say, mister, I couldn't help overhearin' the topic of conversation. Would you have any objection if I went up there right now an' took a look round? I'd try not to get in the way of the man doin' the cleanin'.'

The owner looked anything but interested at first, but one of his cronies whispered something about not missing an opportunity for publicity and this changed his outlook. He beamed rather unexpectedly, reached under the bar and came up with an old spyglass.

'Be my guest, stranger. Stay up there as long as you like. Only don't fall asleep because we do lock and bolt the trapdoor that gives access before we close the saloon.'

Ed thanked him and offered to buy him a beer, which was courteously refused. Feeling a little self-conscious, he set off up the stairs after the cleaner with the spyglass tucked under his arm. The cleaner seemed surprised to see him, but he soon warmed to the idea of company and chatted easily about the town and the goings on in the saloon.

When the bucket of water was dirty the good-hearted fellow went below, promising to bring up another beer for Ed when he returned.

By taking up a position at one of the forward corners of the square tower Ed could see in three directions. He was soon busy with the spyglass, covering the nearest buildings and studying the men who moved among them.

Noon came and went. Conversation with the cleaner grew more difficult. Finally, about half past one in the afternoon, the fellow went below and the need for keeping up conversation was gone.

Left on his own, Ed became more and more impatient. He had come up in the first place on impulse, thinking that he would get a good view of a town he did not know. Now, after a lot of time had passed, he began to think that he had been foolish to act impulsively.

Obviously nothing of a serous nature had happened in the town. He could have explored it on foot for Dan Lawrence and the men he suspected would be with him. He could also have contacted the peace officers in the town and warned them of what he thought might be about to take place. He shrugged. Perhaps his imagination was running away with him. He had nothing to go on in regard to Dan's new companions. Perhaps he had just teamed up with a group of gamblers in order to make a living.

At two o'clock Ed's spirits were very low. He was yawning and wondering if he was going to make a mess of this search he was carrying our for brother Hector. Perhaps, also, he had let down young Dan in his hour of need.

He was frowning and thinking about a search on foot when something familiar caught his eye. It was the tail of a horse. *The* horse which he had been riding for a time. The grey stallion which belonged to Dan Lawrence. Its tail was almost white in colour, and the animal had the habit of flicking it about.

Ed's fingers were slightly unsteady through excitement when he trained the glass on the group of four riders. The grey's present rider was Dan all right. He was wearing a black leather vest now, and a blue bandanna had supplanted his black string tie.

The quartette of mounted men came out of a side turning and turned away from the direction of the saloon to go further east. It was hard to read anything into their expressions, even with the glass. But they looked watchful and acted as though they were a trifle keyed up.

His mind groped towards recognition, but that was slow in coming. A beard and a round black hat were the details which helped him to recall where he had seen the other riders before. It had been outside the saloon in Placerville on the occasion when Dan had dived through a window and then stolen his horse.

He was utterly baffled as to why men who had had marked differences should now be riding along like comrades, but he had a feeling that they were up to no good. And there was another, lesser, consideration. If one of that trio had struck him on the back of the head outside Butler's Ford he wanted to get back at them.

As he sprang towards the trapdoor his friend the cleaner pushed it up and stepped into view with yet another beer, the top inch of which had spilled out on the way up. Ed called him by name.

'Jake, all the time I've been up here I've really been expectin' trouble. I want you to help me. Which way is the peace office from here?'

'Why, Ed, it's about a hundred yards towards the north. But what do you want the peace office for? The marshal usually has his feet up at this time of the day.'

Ed handed over a silver dollar. 'I want you to go to his office and rouse him out. Tell him that you have heard on good authority that there might be a disturbance at the east end of town real soon. If he's curious about me, I'll explain to him later. Will you do it?'

The cleaner, a stooping forty-year-old with a wrinkled skin and few teeth, nodded without enthusiasm. 'If you're sure this ain't some kind of a joke, Ed, I'll go. Sure.'

Ed took him by the shoulders. 'Speed is very important, so get along with you. I'll be along towards the east myself by the time he gets there.'

The detective helped his messenger through the trapdoor, and, after hastily drinking about half the glass of beer, he followed him through and dumped the spyglass on the bar top, heading for the street without waiting to explain.

The buckskin snorted about having been left so long and only showed mild enthusiasm when he cinched up the saddle and sprang on to its back. Ed sent it up the street towards the east. He knew that he was in a difficult position.

If, in fact, he was right about the quartette planning a strike against some building then he would have to act rather carefully, otherwise Dan's last chance of staying on the right side of the law would be jeopardised.

Fifty yards up the street Ed found that his mount was keeping pace with a spritely salesman who was walking along the sidewalk and whistling. He caught his eye, grinned, and addressed a query to him.

'Say, mister, I guess you must know this town better than I do. Is there a bank building up the east end of this street, or have I come the wrong way?'

The salesman nodded. 'Sure, you're on the right course. You want the All-American Third National on the left-hand side. You can almost see it from here. It has that swinging sign with a bison on it over the door.'

Ed touched his hat, thanked him, and moved over to the right side of the street. He was taking advantage of the small amount of shade on that side in case one of the quartette looked back. A couple of minutes later all four horsemen headed their mounts towards a hitch rail a good seventy yards short of the swinging sign.

They sat close together with their heads going this way and that. Ed felt more excited than ever. He had either made a big mistake and they were not going to the bank at all, or else this was the last look round before closing for the strike.

The detective edged his mount in behind a bulky cart with a high canopy. As the vehicle crossed the intersection he turned the buckskin off to the right and made a fairly fast detour down the street parallel with the one he had been using. One line of buildings separated him from the bank and the quartette.

Through a wide alleyway he caught sight of the bank's swinging sign and he knew that he was on a level with the bank. He was also able to ascertain that the Third National and buildings on a level with it were situated on a corner. There was another intersection running across their eastern walls.

The building which lay between Ed and the bank turned out to be a double one. The end facing the bank was a saddler's shop, while the part directly behind it was a livery. The two businesses were back to back.

Ed reined in and dismounted. He

had divested himself of his corduroy jacket, which was strapped to the saddle. He rolled up the sleeves of his blue shirt and adjusted the angle of his hat. His keen ears told him that a group of horses were nearly level with the alley alongside of the double building.

As he did not want to be seen he backtracked past one building, a blacksmith's, and left the buckskin in the alley beside it. So as not to draw too much attention he forced himself to walk back to the saddler's alley. In it was a big grain bin with a sloping lid backed against the livery wall. He used it to hide behind, but soon he was assured that the four riders had gone by and he wanted to be closer to size up the possibilities of cutting out Dan Lawrence from the rest of the outfit.

As he ghosted up the alley to investigate Ed knew what a phenomenal task he had set himself. Dan would most likely behave like the other three, having thrown in his hand with them. If he did, then all he — Ed — could do as a responsible townsman was to raise the alarm, and this was likely to put young Dan in even more trouble than before.

* * *

As the quartette slowed in front of the saddler's shop, Nevada Bill talked to Dan out of the side of his mouth.

'How are your nerves, amigo?'

Dan, who was feeling tremendously excited and a little jumpy, managed a smile which slipped off his face again unbidden. 'I — I guess they'll be all right. Is this where we hitch?'

No one answered him, but the other three all dismounted without haste and looped their reins over the hitch rail in front of the saddler's. Dan rode a yard or so past them and pretended to be toying with his riding gauntlets. Out of his eye corner he saw the trio cross the dirt and pause outside the bank. It had two glass windows which were painted an opaque green almost up to head level.

The trio clustered near the door. The slightest of nods from Nevada Bill sent them forward. As each man passed through the door he pulled up across the lower half of his face a bandanna. Bill favoured black, Hondo's was grey, and Richy's was blue.

The moment the door closed behind them Dan was hit by a strong feeling of loneliness. He felt that he was all alone in the world, that almost anyone could recognise him as a renegade and that he was bound to be accosted before his partners ever got out of the bank again.

A man's idle glance at him made him think that the grey stallion was drawing too much attention. In an effort to divert non-existent attention from the animal and the proximity of the bank he decided to change the laid-down plans ever so slightly.

He sent the grey round the corner of the saddler's shop, moved down the intersection, and rounded the frontage of the livery. The mouth of the alley attracted him and he thought it would be a good idea to leave his mount near the grain bin.

From there he could easily move up the alley and keep watch. He never saw the man who had chosen to hide behind the grain bin and his senses slipped away almost at once when a revolver barrel made contact with the side of his head.

★   ★   ★

Ed was breathing hard. He had not expected Dan to ride all the way into the alley where he himself was hiding. Seeing that Dan had done so he had at once taken advantage of the chance. He had succeeded in cutting out Dan from the rest. Now the young galoot had to be hidden until the goings-on at the bank were all over.

No one came along the street while Dan was propped against the side of the bin. Two minutes later Ed had the lid raised and he was sliding the unconscious body inside. He had tested the fastening of the lid earlier and it was clear that no one had used the bin in many months. He tossed Dan's hat in after him and slammed down the lid. Plenty of air was getting in through a damaged corner and between shrunken planks.

Ed made sure that the grey was secure and then he went up the alley to the danger end. Now that he had Dan safely out of the way he was quite prepared to fire a few angry shots and to make the outlaws' task a difficult one.

At the mouth of the alley he found his hiding place masked by two standing carts. The one in front of the saddler's shop afforded him cover, standing as it did directly between his vantage point and the bank.

He pulled his gun and was about to fire a warning shot or two into the air to give the alarm. He never did this, however, because three gun shots occurred inside the bank and his warning was not necessary.

Nevada Bill's contact was the second teller. The first teller was an old man, slow in his movements and past his best for both seeing and hearing. The bank had recently taken on a brawny lad in his late teens, and it was this youngster who had had the audacity to go for a gun when he thought the trio were too busy attending to the bags they were filling.

The young clerk's bullet had gone over Nevada Bill's head. Nevada had retaliated, shooting the lad in the shoulder. Lamotte had nicked one of two customers in the arm when that person aspired to follow the clerk's example.

The brief fight back gave out as soon as it had started. To further discourage others Hondo hit the second customer over the head and dropped him to the ground, unconscious. Nevada was the first out. He had a gun in one hand and a leather money bag in the other.

Hondo and Lamotte came out together a few seconds later. This far no one in town appeared to have raised the alarm.

Holding up their hands to conceal the fact that they had masks on, the trio started across the dirt. Hondo's eyes showed that he was startled. He had noticed that Dan was missing; also Dan's horse.

Bill shouted: 'Don't bother about him. Get to a horse. He's probably waitin' for us down the street.'

At that moment Ed fired his first angry shot from low under the cart which was hiding him. The bullet from his .45 hit the corner of the bag Nevada was carrying and almost knocked it out of his hand. He shifted his aim and sent a bullet between the second pair of outlaws. They hesitated for a mere second and then returned his fire.

Bullets touched Ed's shirt and hat; so close was their aim he had to move back. He dived for the mouth of the alley again and only narrowly avoided three more bullets all of which chipped chunks out of the corner of the building.

He sucked in air, struggling to get back his breath. In an effort to further impede the outlaws' departure he ran round the livery and entered the intersection. He was only in time to see the hind legs and tail of the bearded man's pinto.

The trio were riding unimpeded up the street in which the bank was located, heading out of town towards the east. Ed emptied his gun after them to no avail. He then sat down on the sidewalk to await the arrival of the peace officers.

15

Town Marshal Ross Sherman, a bulky white-moustached figure with a red face, arrived at the bank some two or three minutes later accompanied by his son Ike, who was also his deputy. They were both out of breath and seemingly rattled by the raid.

The marshal's chest was heaving as he glowered at the group of fifteen to twenty men who had gathered in front of the bank since the raiders left.

He called: 'Which of you gents sent a message for me to come down this end of town? Jake from the saloon came along for me, but he didn't say the bank was about to be robbed.'

A neat dapper man with a hold-all in his hand threaded his way through the crowd of watchers and entered the Third National with a purposeful step. This was the town's doctor, who had rightly anticipated trouble.

Ed stood up slowly. He had been reloading his weapon. 'I was the one who sent a message to you, marshal, but I couldn't say exactly what to expect because I was only working on instinct. I saw these men go up the street. I was watching them through a spyglass at the time. There was jest something in the way they were conducting themselves which made me suspicious. I regret I didn't get up here a little sooner myself.'

'Who are you, stranger?'

'The name is Ed Morissey. I come from Silver Creek. I've seen those three men before one time. In Placerville. They were outside a saloon after a disturbance. I could give you a description if you like.'

'I do like, an' I'd like for you to step over into the bank, Mr. Morissey.'

The crowd gave way for the two peace officers and Ed to enter the bank. All three of them looked around, their glances full of curiosity. The doctor, an efficient fellow at his craft, had the young clerk stretched out on the counter. He was in the act of extracting the bullet from his shoulder.

Holding the youth down were the other two tellers. One was an old man and the other a startled-looking man with eroded eyes and lined cheeks. The manager, a small bespectacled man in his shirt sleeves, was endeavouring to bathe and bandage the arm of the wounded client.

The man who had been pistol-whipped was bathing his head wth water out of the same basin.

'Don't ask me how much we lost, marshal. I'd say at a guess between thirty and forty thousand! Is there any chance of giving chase to the bank's money?'

The manager had looked up from his first aid. Marshal Sherman, who had been touched on a raw spot by the remark, glanced at his son and then at Ed. 'You know how reluctant men from this town are to give chase to renegades, manager. All I can do is inform the county authorities an' hope they can do something.'

The bank manager sniffed with great fervour. He turned his back on the peace officers, apparently washing his hands of them.

Sherman said: 'Take down some details about the raiders. As soon as you can I want you to telegraph the county sheriff an' tell him what has happened, son. Mr. Morissey, here, looks to me like a good witness.'

The bruised client mentioned in a loud voice what a pity it was that the county seat was in the opposite direction to where the raiders had gone, but the peace officers ignored it.

Ed gave as full a description as he could of the three men who had been riding with Dan. He was quite clear about the details he had observed and only showed some doubt when it came to describing the mounts of Collins and Lamotte. He gave it as his opinion that they were riding a sorrel and a roan, which, although he did not know it, was quite accurate.

As soon as he had finished Ed made excuses about feeling thirsty and wandered out into the street. He was far from being fully at ease. This far no one had come forward to say that there were four horses at one time and only three had ridden away from the bank. No one was asking for the fourth man.

Ed had visions of Dan slowly reviving and pounding the sides of the grain bin to get out. If he did and anyone who was suspicious came around to free him, there was a chance that he might just say something accidentally which might incriminate him.

He reminded himself that Dan was a redhead and at times very headstrong. Perhaps he would object to being helped in so forceful a fashion. Ed really was thirsty, but as he crossed the top of the alley where he had hidden himself he saw a liveryman inspecting the grey stallion only a few paces from the grain bin.

Perspiration broke out on his brow. Instead of making for the nearest drinking den he hurried towards the ostler and put on a bold face. 'I wonder if you'd be good enough to take that horse into your stable for me? It belongs to a pardner of mine who ducked out when the shootin' started. I'd like for you to give the animal a groomin' and a light feed.

'My horse is up the next alley. It could do with the same treatment. If you've got the time to see to the pair of them I'll be glad to fetch mine along.'

The ostler, a broad-faced veteran of sixty summers, eyed Ed up and down and then beamed. 'I guess you must be the young hombre who was doin' the shootin' a while back. Kind of hot while it lasted, wasn't it? Sure, I'll be glad to see to the two horses for you. Leave the other one to me if you like. I'll collect it.'

Ed beamed in his turn. 'That sure is mighty helpful of you, mister. I'll leave them both to you then.'

231

He turned on his heel and began to walk back up the alley, but as soon as the ostler had gone to fetch the buckskin he dodged back again and put his face against the lid of the bin.

'Hey, you in there!' he began in a loud whisper. 'You stay quite still an' quiet till I come for you. Understand? If anyone sees you come out of there you'll go to the penitentiary for bank robbery.'

Without waiting for an answer, he darted off up the alley and almost ran to the saloon.

* * *

When Ed raised the lid of the grain bin a half hour after nightfall he found Dan sitting up inside it and fingering a promising contusion on the side of his head. The young detective did not bother to re-introduce himself. He merely glowered down at the fellow for whom he had taken so many chances.

'My, my, Pearl Winder sure would get

a surprise if she could see you now. Witness Daniel Lawrence, the last of the great bank raiders. I don't think.'

Dan started to smell what Ed had brought with him. He remarked: 'I don't suppose you've gone to a deal of trouble jest to mock me in my hour of need. Is that food I can smell?'

'Yes, beans and cabbage and beef, and fruit pie an' coffee. But you don't get any of it to eat until you promise me that you will do things my way from now on.'

Dan got as far as his knees. He appeared to be sniffing the air like a cat in a strange area. He was hearing the noises of late evening, and after being confined for so long it was hard to believe that the forces of law and order were not actively engaged in looking for him.

'All right, Ed, I'll do things your way. Though why you should go to so much trouble after the way you've been treated I can't rightly understand. Did you bring any eatin' irons?'

Ed yanked him out of the bin. The lid was quietly lowered and it served for a table even though it had a slant. Dan had never tasted food so good. He was hungry, more so than he could remember for a long time. He wanted to ask questions as to how the raid had gone, but the effort of filling his face precluded talk for a time.

He was almost out of breath through the speedy mastication of food when the last of the coffee was consumed.

'What do we do now?' he asked tentatively.

'We collect the horses an' we ride right on out of this town an' give thanks that neither bank raiders nor peace officers are breathin' down your neck. It ain't too late for some half-drunk townsman to happen along an' say there was a fourth man in the bank raid. An' you perched up on that grey of yours looked pretty conspicuous when I was on the lookout.'

Dan waited patiently while Ed returned the eating gear. He cooled his heels a little longer while the two horses were collected, but he had no criticism to offer when Ed headed them in a southerly direction rather than to east or west.

* * *

That night they slept out in the open well away from any settlements. Dan was puzzled about this, but he had given his word that he would not question Ed's plans so he did not argue about it. Had he done so he might have been told quite bluntly that Ed was not yet fully convinced of his change of heart.

The young detective had a feeling that if they came too soon to a town Dan might be tempted to make off again. Throughout the following day they had no contact with anyone connected with Hardrock Springs and the bank raid. Dan had told what he knew about the outlaws' movements after leaving the town. As the hours went by Ed was lulled into an overdue sense of security. If Nevada Bill had kept to his plans then he and his two sidekicks would be well to the north-east of the terrain over which the two partners were riding.

Late in the afternoon the peaceful-ness of lush foliage on the south side of a wide, placid, waterway made them think of home and the events that had taken place since Dan's return from law school.

They rode slowly westward on an undulating path one behind the other with Dan leading. The drooping branches of weeping willows at times brushed them and their horses down the right side. Ed felt prompted to ask a ques-tion, the answer to which meant a whole lot to him. He thought the time was ripe to ask it.

His eyes were shaded by the substan-tial brim of his hat. 'Dan, can you answer me this? Are you in love with Pearl Winder? I figure you owe me something, an' I'd like the truth.'

Dan turned in the saddle. He was taking the question very seriously and wondering at the same time about Ed's feelings in the matter. What happened next, however, blasted the subject right out of his mind. From across the water, some seventy yards away, three rifles suddenly started shooting from cover.

Dan was lucky, because the grey carried him into rock cover in one stride, but Ed was not so fortunate. A ricochet just touched the buckskin's rump so that it lunged suddenly sideways and unintentionally threw him. The fair man slid smoothly towards the earth, but unfortunately his head connected with a rock on the way down and this robbed him of his senses.

The buckskin backed off away from the water, coming to rest in a small hollow, while Dan dismounted and drew his Henry, licking his lips and wondering whether he was capable of keeping the three hostile guns on the far side of the water. The young lawyer knew that his loyalty to Ed was being put to the test. At first he had nothing at all to indicate that the hostile guns were his former associates, but he felt it in his bones.

The trio stopped shooting as both their targets had gone out of sight. Meanwhile Dan, who could just see the lower half of Ed's inert form amid lush fern and grass, waited with his rifle resting on a rock partially screened by creek bank foliage. He did not have long to wait.

The trees on the north bank, which had been apparently empty, soon showed the forms of three men on horseback. The briefest examination with the naked eye showed who they were. Nevada edged his sorrel nearer the water's edge prior to jumping it into the creek.

Dan took aim against him with his teeth lightly clenched. He could not see himself deliberately shooting down a man he had ridden with, but he was determined to stop the trio from crossing, if he could, for Ed's sake.

He aimed his rifle between the sorrel's front hooves and squeezed the trigger. The fine reddish-brown animal reared in alarm. Dan noted this, but he had two others to dissuade, so he did the same again. First Lamotte and then Mercer suffered the same treatment. As the echoes died away the trio and their horses disappeared from view.

Nevada called: 'Lawrence, if that's you shooting, you've just signed your own death warrant!'

Dan figured that talking was a change from exchanging bullets, so he replied. This far there was no sign of Ed's returning to consciousness. He had to win time and every minute might count in a situation like this.

'This is me, Dan Lawrence! Why don't you three go on your way an' spend your ill-gotten gains? You don't give a hang about me! I'd let you down sooner or later.'

There was an animated exchange between the three men before Nevada started to answer Dan.

He shouted: 'For a lawyer, amigo, you ain't all that bright. Me, I've never yet been careless enough to get my name an' description on a reward dodger. So will you tell me how I can let you live knowin' what you do about me an' my boys?'

The last word had scarcely been uttered when the guns of Mercer and Lamotte opened up on the rock behind which Dan was standing. He was shaken when chips of rock flew in his face. He ducked well down and wondered what was to be done. Ed's hand on his shoulder about a minute later almost shocked him as badly.

Ed gripped his hand and shook it. There was little need for a discussion of the present situation. The detective was now satisfied that Dan had permanently thrown in his lot with him.

'Dan, I'll have to wait for the answer to that question. Right now we ought to pull out. We can't keep those jaspers on the other side of the water all day. Are you ready?'

Dan nodded tight-lipped. He undertook to collect the two horses while Ed kept watch on the other bank. One outlaw put up his stetson on a stick. It was blasted off within a few seconds by the detective's Winchester.

Five minutes later, the two young men withdrew. They mounted up and rode off at a good speed towards the west. The waterway continued to meander between them and their pursuers, but they knew that they dare not ease up or relax.

Ed felt some relief when his head cleared.

16

The protracted horse trek west went on for upwards of four hours, with very few let-ups for drinks and refreshments. During the ride the partners talked spasmodically. After the clash in the afternoon Ed knew only too well that the trio they had temporarily repulsed would be back on their trail with the minimum of delay.

The night halt was liable to be a critical time for the two of them. If they survived until daylight their chances of getting back to Silver Creek unscathed would improve.

Consequently, it was of the utmost importance to choose carefully a place to bed down.

Ed said more than once, 'It has to be an obvious-looking place where we can turn the tables. Where we can defend ourselves and also attack. A lot of lead will be thrown during the dark hours, an' if you entertain any notions of simply aimin' to scare people off, Dan, we'll both likely be buzzard bait before dawn.'

'I know what you mean, an' I know you speak good sense, Ed. I think I'll be able to do the necessary when the time comes. After all the trouble you've taken I don't want to give them the chance of their revenge.'

Around a quarter past eight, when their water canteens were almost empty and they were becoming nervous again through continued pressure, Dan's spirits began to rise a little. He had begun to recognise certain landmarks which he had seen earlier when the outlaw outfit was resting up outside of Butler's Ford.

With the beginnings of the dried-out waterway, the young redhead found himself smiling and nodding. He kept his eyes averted from Ed when he spoke. 'About that earlier question, I've been thinkin' quite a lot an' I've come to the conclusion that I don't love Pearl Winder. I simply came back to town, found she was about the prettiest eligible girl, and I liked goin' around with her. If we make it back there'll be changes, of course. Her Pa will see to that.'

Ed made a noise which implied that he had heard and understood what had been said, but for once he had no comment to offer. He was simply feeling an intense, though embarrassing, relief.

'Back to business,' Dan went on hurriedly. 'This gully is quite a useful one. It's dry now, but there are patches where water can be coaxed out with a little effort. I'd like for us to move a little further north on to harder ground. The gully turns north within half a mile an' I think I can show you a place such as we need to camp on.'

They rode on until the gully barred their way. From the trees on the top of the bank they could see sandy patches of a different colour. Obviously water was not far below the surface. Dan was the first to head down into the sandy expanse and go to work with a tool.

Ed waited on the higher ground, studying the facilities which nature provided for a gunfight against odds. Working with renewed energy, they produced water and built a fire within a few feet of it, in the centre of the gully.

The young detective finished his food first and went north a few yards to dig another hole exclusively for the horses. Some fifteen minutes later they had argued out exactly where they were going to be when the opposition overtook them.

Each needed a commanding position for retaliation against guns firing down upon the bedrolls beside the fire. Prominently placed on the west bank were three age-old grey rocks which would do for one such position. The other key point was amid larger rocks delicately balanced on a large, low, flat outcrop. This position was on the eastern bank and further up the gully by about thirty-odd yards, opposite the horses' waterhole and the place where the animals were to bed down.

The rigging of the bedrolls took a good five minutes. The blankets had to be made to look as if they contained bodies. This was achieved by an adroit use of hats and saddles. An odd weapon would have been a final touch, but they could not spare those.

Ed elected to fight from the outcrop as he was a fair shot with his Winchester. Dan had no complaints when he was assigned to the rocks on the west bank. They retired to these two positions early and did what they could to make themselves comfortable during the trying waiting period.

★　★　★

The fading daylight seemed too slow to depart. Twilight played tricks with their eyes. For a long time their ears told them nothing of other men approaching their prepared positions. Both Ed and

Dan were frequently on the verge of deep sleep before a slight restlessness on the part of the horses warned them that something was afoot.

Very gradually they became aware of slight sounds following the near side of the gully as it went through the slow curve, changing its direction from west to north. There was a puzzling pause at a good distance which was difficult to interpret in movement. Later it was to become clear what was the outlaws' special move.

Finally the faint noises seemed to settle amid the trees on the east bank, in the place where Ed had first examined the camp site. Five minutes' agony of suspense was terminated by a sudden fusillade of rifle fire from the trees.

Bullets ripped into both bedrolls, displacing the hats and throwing the whole area into disarray. While the hostile gun muzzles were still putting up brief flashes of flame Ed fired into the area from which they came. At one time he thought he heard a human cry, but he could not be sure.

After the first flurry of shooting from the bank and the outcrop another rifle opened up on the west bank, further south than Dan's position. Again the bedrolls were the targets. As soon as this gun started to fire Dan, who had been dozing when the first shots occurred, turned his gun against the source of the latest shots and fired steadily.

There was no more firing from the outlaw who had earlier crossed the gully. One of the original pair of attackers must have survived because a single rifle briefly probed Dan's position. Dan, however, did not fire back and gradually the awful period of waiting for daylight began.

Faint sounds floated around the area after an hour or two, but they were difficult to interpret. No one moved in the early dawn, and Ed and Dan were chilled and edgy by the time they decided to show themselves and risk an attack from someone with more patience.

Ed discovered the body of Hondo Mercer among the trees. He had been shot through the side of the head. There was no sign of the man who had been with him, or the horses which had brought them.

On Dan's side of the gully they found Richy Lamotte, who had died slowly from a chest wound. His horse had wandered away. While they cooked breakfast over the fire Dan explained a few more details about them.

He went on: 'The survivor is the most deadly of the three of them, a man named Nevada Bill Collins, who seems more intent upon eliminating me than on going away to spend his loot. I rather figure that he won't give up. How do you see it?'

Ed gave a wry smile. 'It's either him or us, amigo. We'll meet again all right. We'll have to keep on the alert all the time or else he'll bush-whack us. So let's get our chores done. As soon as we've finished eatin' we'll bury these two outlaws an' then move on.'

As they dug the burial hole they could not help wondering who would be next in line for a planting.

★ ★ ★

The morning was well advanced when Nevada Bill reined in at the southernmost projection of a sprawling hogsback ridge which lay approximately north and south in direction. He had traversed about ten miles from the scene of the abortive ambush, and now his first concern was to give his sorrel a rest and switch his weight to Hondo's pinto.

The two-coloured horse was a bad-tempered beast at times, but it had stamina and it was very surefooted. Its surefootedness gave him an idea. He studied the outlandish ridge all over again and wondered whether he could use it for his special purpose. The two men who had killed his sidekicks were almost certain to come that way.

If he could kill them from a natural spur on the ridge, or lure them into a risky climb on to the heights after him, then, surely, he stood a good chance of eliminating them both. He had no sooner considered the idea than he started to climb.

The spur he was heading for up the winding track was some two hundred feet above the valley floor. From the northern end of it an animal track led upwards again to a broad saddle-like pass, which gave access to the eastern side of the mass.

With the pinto under him and the sorrel in tow he kept his confidence and made steady progress.

* ★ *

The rifle winked light on the spur while the two riding partners were still considering the magnificence of the view. Ed was the first to notice. He slipped his left stirrup and urgently kicked the rump of Dan's grey.

251

The first bullet went between them. Dan leapt the stallion into timber cover and kept on going. A second shot ricochetted off a trail rock and slightly burned the outside of Ed's thigh. He flinched and sprang sideways out of the saddle, finding cover, but jarring his chest a little on trailside rocks.

The buckskin snickered and went off through the rocks towards a thin patch of scrub at the southernmost tip of the ridge.

Dan began to fire back at the spur. Within a few minutes the head and shoulders of Nevada showed briefly as he left his vantage point and started up the higher track towards the pass. Masking rock made his movements safe for a while.

Still on horseback, Dan came back through the thinning timber to find out what had happened to Ed. They called to one another while the redhead continued to keep track of Nevada's advance.

'Are you wounded, Ed? Tell me straight.'

'I've got a very slight nick on the thigh. Hardly anything to show really. What is your ex-buddy doin'?'

'He's moved up. Looks to be headin' for the saddle, the way through to the other side. What do we do now?'

'Do you feel up to chasin' him to the saddle, up the path on this side? It would be dangerous.'

'What would you do if I did?'

'Mount up with the least possible delay, ride round the ridge an' try to get him as he came out on the other side. I could do it, too, if you kept his attention for a while. What do you say?'

Dan answered without hesitation. 'I'll do it. Do you want any help to get back to horse?'

Ed said that he could manage and told Dan to make sure that Nevada knew he was following up behind. Almost at once he was on his feet and running through the rocks and scrub to where he expected to find the buckskin.

Suddenly, speed had become an essential part of the plan. Ed found the horse, mounted up, and rode off around the other side of the ridge at a good speed. A few sharp glances as he pushed on served to assure him that Nevada had not reached the saddle. He watched that point most of the time while the labouring buckskin took him to the foot of the winding path below it.

When he was about a third of the way up the path he heard a sharp exchange of gun shots. He paused for about half a minute, wondering if there had been a casualty, and then he pressed on again.

The crucial time came about ten minutes later. Ed was then considerably further up the side of the ridge, but the going was not easy. A fairly narrow path with a vertical cliff on the inner side made progress difficult. To make matters worse, he had been holding his thigh in a special position and this had made it ache in the region of the slight groove.

There was an echoing ring of hooves in the saddle as Nevada came clattering through it. Ed's heart thumped with excitement. The outlaw appeared to have survived the last exchange. But would he be in such a rush if Dan were dead? It was most unlikely.

In coming through so fast the outlaw either wanted to get down the other side rather quickly or else he was planning an ambush as Dan followed him through the narrow pass.

Nevada came forward and examined the slope. His brows rose in surprise when he noted where the top of Ed's hat showed. One bullet, however, was all he sent down at the bobbing target, and that missed. Small pieces of earth flew around Ed's head, but he pressed on.

His mind was very busy. He calculated that Dan was about to show himself and enter the ambush in the next three minutes. In that time he — Ed — would not have climbed far enough to be able to fire a telling shot at the ambusher. The cliff on the inner side of the track was too high.

Ed fought down his angry frustration and came up with an idea. If anything went wrong it might amount almost to suicide. But, having struggled for so long to get Dan back to Silver Creek in one piece, he felt that a calculated personal risk was worthwhile.

He cautiously flexed his left thigh, found that it worked freely enough, and decided to go through with his perilous stunt. One glance away to his right was almost enough to put him off. Any sort of a fall down there was certain to result in multiple injuries at the very least.

He pushed such thoughts out of his mind, hauled out his Winchester, and scanned the heights above him. He could not see what he wanted for the cliff top. Licking his lips, he eased out of the stirrups and cautiously knelt across the saddle. Two yards further on he noticed a slight movement through the grasses and roots. It was not a horse.

He checked the buckskin, ordered it to keep still, and, in that position, he slowly straightened up, with perspiration beading his forehead. His knees trembled, but he managed to raise the gun into a shooting position.

Nevada's head, small and insignificant beyond the gun-sight, looked very much alive. In fact the head was seen in profile. Nevada was looking along his own gun, training it on the pass.

Ed checked his aim very carefully and squeezed the trigger. The gun fired. Slight movement made him lose his balance. He bent and dropped in a forked position over the saddle, grabbing a protruding tree root with his left hand. Soil and rubble pattered away from under the buckskin's hooves, but the animal somehow contrived to stay calm and still.

A long drawn out cry preceded the reappearance of Nevada Bill. He was wounded and his falling body abruptly appeared up above and began to fall down the steep hillside, bouncing infrequently.

Ed, who was still forked across the buckskin's back, caught an unusual upside down view of his passing which lasted only a second. The unfortunate renegade parted from his weapon and his hat before finally coming to rest at the foot of the ridge with all the life knocked out of him.

Ed and Dan found him a half-hour later. They took a long-awaited rest before attempting to bury his remains.

★ ★ ★

A furlong short of Silver Creek, at two in the afternoon a couple of days later, the detective and his charge pulled up for a short halt. They had come a long way in company and now that they were about to re-enter their home town they wanted to spruce themselves up a bit.

They changed their shirts, knocked

the dust out of their hats, coats and trousers, and dusted their boots.

When they were about ready Dan became unduly silent. Asked what was the matter, he tried to shrug off his mood without success.

'These last few days in your company, Ed, have been different. A sort of interim period between towns, between lives almost. Now, when I get back, I'll be on my own again. I've got to face up to things. The folks of Silver Creek won't welcome the likes of me back again. The only twinkle will be in the eye of your brother. You'll see.'

Ed seemed troubled. He said that he hoped that the atmosphere in town would not be as cold as all that. As they mounted up again and took their two ownerless horses in tow he could not help sharing Dan's apprehensiveness. Nor could he help wondering what sort of thoughts would first go through the head of pretty Pearl Winder when she heard that the two of them had returned.

Almost as soon as they entered the outskirts they became aware of a certain suppressed excitement. At first it was hard to understand. Dan kept his head down as nodding acquaintances and strangers began to peer at him. Ed touched his hat a few times, but he was also puzzled.

Small boys ran after them laughing and waving. One of them with a high-pitched voice yelled: 'Hey, you two! Have you heard about Slim Burns?'

A man who was passing waved a fist at the child and succeeded in stemming the flow of words before an explanation could be shouted.

As they entered Main Street, Dan asked: 'Who's Slim Burns, Ed?'

'Why, he's that rather good-looking young blacksmith's striker. Lives with his sister on the outskirts of town. The sister is courting one of the store clerks, I think.'

Dan nodded and lost interest. The more he withdrew into himself the more passers-by seemed to show interest. Ed increased the pace of his mount and drew Dan after him. They did not pause until they were outside the office of Hector Morissey. At the same time Hector himself came round the side of the building and stood for a moment blinking with surprise. And then he beamed. Ed noted that he looked fit and relaxed and by far the most self-assured of the three of them. Surely Hector could not have known that they were coming. The date was only a few days off the critical time when Dan was supposed to show himself again to defend the charge in the Skinner Kopak case.

Hector waited for them to dismount and ushered them through to his private office with a magnanimous gesture. When they were seated he handed out cigars. Dan took his as though it was a special privilege for a condemned man.

Hector began: 'Nice to see you, boys. There's a funeral in town this after-noon. You won't have heard, but young

Slim Burns died yesterday. An accident. A horse kicked him and he died about twenty minutes later.'

Ed smoked poker-faced, and Dan merely glowered at his employer.

'Before Slim died he owned up to the killing of Skinner Kopak with your gun, Dan. It seems he thought Skinner was seeing too much of his sister when she was out courting with her young man. So Slim acted on a sudden impulse and shot him with the borrowed gun.

'The last thing he said before he died was that he was sorry for the trouble he had apparently caused you. His confession means that you don't have any proper charge to face in the Kopak case. All you have to do is show yourself. As for that other incident in the saloon. No one ever seriously thought of blaming you for that. So everything is fine an' dandy. So long as you don't go off again.'

Several minutes elapsed before Dan's depression finally lifted. He said his thanks and asked permission to be free of work until the next day. He then left, but he did not go visiting. He simply went to his quarters and started on a long bout of sleep.

Ed stayed in the office and explained much of what had happened. Before he left Hector paid him a substantial sum of money for his services.

★　★　★

After the funeral Ed repeated a good deal of the information about the robbers of the Hardrock Springs bank to Marshal Dick Speed, who was interested to know that they had been eliminated and rather disappointed because the whereabouts of the loot was not known.

At a later hour Ed was standing smoking in front of his own office when the parents of Pearl Winder went by in their buggy. He straightened himself up and touched his hat through force of habit, not expecting much of a response. To his surprise, however, the old man slowed his horses and returned the hat salute. And before the conveyance moved again Mrs. Winder had beamed at him and shouted an invitation:

'When you've had time to rest up, Ed, do ride out our way an' take a bite to eat with us. We'd love to hear how you an' Dan made out on your travels! Goodbye!'

Ed was so surprised he dropped his cigarette. Instead of retrieving it he rubbed his heel on it. It appeared that the Winders knew he and Dan had come back together and, in spite of Dan's exoneration, they wanted to hear the story of their exploits from *him*.

This augured well for a man who pined for Pearl's company. He went indoors and set out his shaving kit. Maybe that evening would not be too early to call.

We do hope that you have enjoyed reading this large print book.

Did you know that all of our titles are available for purchase?

We publish a wide range of high quality large print books including:
**Romances, Mysteries, Classics General Fiction
Non Fiction and Westerns**

Special interest titles available in large print are:
**The Little Oxford Dictionary
Music Book, Song Book
Hymn Book, Service Book**

Also available from us courtesy of Oxford University Press:
**Young Readers' Dictionary
(large print edition)
Young Readers' Thesaurus
(large print edition)**

For further information or a free brochure, please contact us at:
**Ulverscroft Large Print Books Ltd.,
The Green, Bradgate Road, Anstey,
Leicester, LE7 7FU, England.
Tel:** (00 44) **0116 236 4325
Fax:** (00 44) **0116 234 0205**

Other titles in the
Linford Western Library:

NEVADA HAWK

Hank J. Kirby

The long trail ended at Castle Rock in New Mexico Territory. Nevada found the man who had murdered his wife — then killed him as he'd planned. What was the next step now? A talented gunman like Nevada was always in demand. He didn't care what type of work he took on, or how dangerous. Life — his own, that is — no longer mattered much any more. Or did it . . . ? He would breathe plenty of gunsmoke before he found the answer.